Sapphire

RARE GEMS SERIES BOOK 1

BY

KATHI S. BARTON

World Castle Publishing, LLC

WCP
World Castle Publishing, LLC
Pensacola, Florida

Copyright © Kathi S. Barton 2013
ISBN: 9781629890043
First Edition World Castle Publishing, LLC October 1, 2013
http://www.worldcastlepublishing.com

Licensing Notes

Cover: Karen Fuller
Photos: Shutterstock
Editor: Eric Johnston

Chapter 1

The house was not only too big, but fucking huge. She walked around the front of it, then around to the back, and didn't really see any improvement on the size. What the hell had she been thinking buying a house this flipping big, sight unseen? Sapphire looked around to her grandmother when she came up beside her.

"It's a monstrosity, isn't it?" her grandmother said and looked up as she continued. "The land is nice, but oh, my Sapphire, how on earth are we going to heat this thing in the winter months, not to mention keep cool in the summer?"

Sapphire had been thinking the same thing. And even though she and her family didn't need a great deal of heat, some was better than none at all. But this thing? She might have to dip into her savings a bit more before it was finished. Not that she minded all that much…they were finally safe.

"I've talked to the local pack last week when I got here. He's a shit. Told me that I was going to be put to the kitchens when the meetings were held." Her grandmother snorted as she continued berating the new alpha. "Arrogant ass. I told him we'd be to the mandatory meetings, but we were only telling him we were in the area, not becoming a part of his whole."

"I bet that went over well," Sapphire said as she followed her grandmother to the front of the house again when they heard the truck pulling up the drive. "I guess we'll be moving in now. I hope the rest of them will be more help unloading than they were loading this sucker."

"They will be. I put the fear of me in them last night. Once they realized I was serious, all of them agreed that they'd be helpful." Sapphire laughed at her grandmother's threat, then took a good look at her. She looked like she might blow away in good wind, but she was tough as nails. Her sisters spilled out of the house just as the driver was getting out.

"You Sapphire Erickson?" the man called. She nodded at the man. "The other truck is behind me about an hour. He got himself stuck in that turnpike and didn't get off when I told him. Stupid kid."

He opened the back end up and all of them looked inside. Who would have thought they could have so much in that tiny little house they'd lived in before coming here? And there was still another truck to come. Smiling, she thought of all the crap they'd left behind.

Her sisters did help unload. It was hot and they bitched a great deal, but mostly it was because they were fighting over which rooms they wanted. Sapphire had already decided she didn't really care where she slept so long as her bed fit in the room. She'd gotten used to her super king and wasn't giving it up for anyone. So when she was directed to the upper level with her mattress, she thought they were doing it to get back at her for buying this house, but when she entered the room was just what she would have picked for herself.

"Like it?" a voice asked from behind her. She turned to look at Jade after the truck pulled away and they were assigned to fix their beds. "I'm just down the hall. You and I are the only two on this floor. The rest of them decided to stay on the lower levels. I don't think I've ever seen a four-story house before."

"It was cheap and big," Sapphire replied. "Plus the yard and woods behind us come with it." She looked around the room and loved it even with all the boxes and furniture haphazardly put everywhere. "Do you have the same view? I can't wait until tonight to see if I can see the moon as clearly as we can the trees."

"Yeah, but not as large as yours. You have the best room, and me...well, come on down and I'll show you." Sapphire followed her sister down the hall and could hear someone coming up. She looked over the circling staircase and saw the others coming toward them. All of her sisters seemed to have something they were trying their best to hide.

"What's going on?" Sapphire demanded. Jade shrugged and stood outside her room. "Jade, what the hell is going on? You know how much I hate not knowing everything."

"I do. That's why this was so hard for me and the others. And you'd better be nice when this goes down, or so help me, I'll feed you something to make you bloat up like a woman on PMS." Sapphire looked at her sisters coming down the hall, then back at Jade. "Behave."

"We love the house," Opal, one of her sisters, said. Sapphire nodded at her, still not sure what the hell was going on. "We got you something. Something for your room to say thanks. Please don't be pissy about it."

Sapphire felt a pain in her heart. Two people—two people that she loved more than anything—had just told her to be nice. When had she...she supposed she had been a little stressed lately with the move and other things going on, but it hadn't been that bad, had it? Then she looked at the small gifts that they were holding out to her, and all she could think about was money wasted. She didn't reach for the gifts right away as she thought about what she'd just had run through her mind. Christ, she was horrible.

"I'm glad.... I'm really glad you like it. I was...I was afraid that you'd all hate it and would want to...." She took a deep breath and looked at her sisters. "Have I really been so horrible? No, don't answer that. I have been. I'm really...I'm really sorry."

She moved down the hall toward her room, intending to go inside and lock the door. She was fighting the tears hard, and she didn't want to break down in front of them. Before she could get the door opened, she felt a hand on her shoulder and turned to her grandmother.

"Hiding won't settle this and you know it," her grandmother said. Sapphire nodded. "Then if you understand that, I want you to get your ass back there and hug them. You need them, and they need you more than ever before. You can be a little human for once."

"I'm not a nice person," Sapphire lamented, but her grandmother just shook her head. "I'm not. And the worst part of it is I don't know if I want to change. I hurt so badly."

"Of course you do." She turned to look at Ruby as she pulled her into her arms. "Christ, he was a fucking asshole, and you should have listened to me when I told you he was a jerk."

Sapphire laughed and looked at the rest of them. Diamond, Jade, Ruby, and Emerald stood with her and

4

Opal. Her father called them his gems, his rare gems. Sapphire took the gifts then and held them to her.

"I'm not going to change, you know. I'm still going to be a pain in all your asses," Sapphire said. Diamond groaned, and the rest laughed. "I mean it. New house, but the same rules apply. We have to…Grandmother said the pack alpha is a prick, so we'll have to be on our guard. You know what happened before."

They'd been the target of the alpha when he decided that giving them to his men would be a good way to break them in before they met their mates. But that hadn't been all he'd tried. He'd tried to hurt them just to get back at her, and she'd found out. Almost too late, too. Sapphire had nearly killed Jeffery Benetton, the alpha, that night, and she and her sisters were hunted for nearly the entire time she looked for this house. Jeffery thought it was his duty to bring her to heel; all of them, including their grandmother, so that whatever reasons he had to make her miserable were justified in his mind. Well, fuck his pack now.

"Do you think he'll come here?" Emerald asked. Sapphire started to tell her no, but really wasn't sure. "I mean, we didn't really hide the fact that we were leaving. But he really didn't give us much of a choice, either."

"No, he didn't, but I would assume he will get the hint and leave us alone. I'm going to meet with the alpha tomorrow to see what he thinks is going to happen now that we're here. I don't know what he'll say about us, but fuck him, too." She looked at her sisters. "I'll protect you with my life. You know that, right?"

"Yes, you moron, we know you're all bad assed and all." Ruby laughed and turned to the stairs. "The truck is here. And the sooner we get this sucker unpacked the sooner we can order pizza. I'm starved."

As they went down the stairs, Sapphire opened her room up and put her gifts on the dresser. There in the middle of her mattress was a large box with a big pink bow on it. She tore the paper off and laughed out loud when she saw what was in the box. She was going to have to have a talk with Diamond. The woman was just too much.

But as she went down the stairs she wondered about the toys her sister had given her, and wondered maybe if she used them she'd be a bit more relaxed. A vibrator would probably be less stressful than a man right now.

The truck took them nearly five hours to unload. Tempers were much more relaxed this time, and the young man who had driven this load helped them. The other man had sat on the porch and complained about how hot it was. She invited Tim to stay for pizza with them.

"No thanks, miss. I have to be getting back. I'm real sorry again I was so late. The directions he gave me were very…wrong." He handed her the paper, and she could see right away that the person who had written them had written the wrong exit. It was a small wonder the man ever got there. "I had my phone and the GPS on it. I don't know what I would have done if he had written down the wrong address, too."

She gave him a fifty dollar tip, and he gushed over that for five minutes before he got in the big semi and left. Sapphire went into the house to start moving the furniture in the dining room to where they wanted it. She was glad now that she'd bought the big house. It meant they could all live together.

Each sister was to take a room. It wasn't as if they needed much in the way of help moving the furniture. All of them had superhuman strength as wolves, but the thing that set them apart from most females in any pack was that they were independent, too…much too independent to want to wait for a big, strong man to move things around. They simply did it themselves and said screw waiting around. Their grandmother had taught them that.

"Do you suppose the garden out back will produce more than some weeds?" her grandmother said. Sapphire laughed and turned to her grandmother as she sat in one of the chairs she'd just set around the large table. "I would love to grow some vegetables, though why I have no idea since none of you eat them."

"I like grilled vegetables. And the guy I bought this place from said he'd come out and turn the ground for you if you wanted him to. He told me that he and his wife grew a nice garden and sold some of it to the locals. You thinking of trying your hand at that?"

"Would be nice for the extra income. Give me some pocket money, too." She reached for the centerpiece and started fussing with it. "I was wondering if you've given any thought to the job offer."

She had, a great deal as a matter of fact, but she was no closer to knowing if she should take it or not. "I would have to be gone most of the day. And you would have to pick up the slack around here. I know we're all supposed to be adults and all, but Emerald and Ruby won't finish college if you don't make them go."

"I've thought of that, too. And I can make them attend. I know that Emerald is excited about being somewhere new, and Ruby was looking at the paper when I came in here to see if she could start her internship somewhere close. I think that sounds promising."

Sapphire thought so, too. Her younger sisters hadn't been all that happy with the situation at their other place, as the alpha had made things difficult for them. Education for women was not high on his list of things that he wanted.

"Emerald and Ruby both are in their last year, so maybe they'll be okay," Sapphire said. Grandmother nodded but fussed with the plant more. "Okay, spill it. You hate that thing, and all that tweaking is not going to make it look any better."

"This was a wedding present from someone when I married your grandfather. Have some respect." She shoved it away. "I'm throwing it out the next trash day. But I do have a concern. Not about the house, though. As I've said, it's going to be expensive to maintain, but we'll manage. I'm concerned about you."

"Me? There's nothing wrong with me. I'm just fine." Sure she was, she thought. And monkeys had feathers. "I told you before that the wounds have healed well and I'm getting stronger all the time."

Which was a flat-out lie. She knew it, and so did her grandmother. The wounds would never heal if she didn't pledge to a new alpha or take a mate...not really much of an option since she was never doing either. She'd rather hurt physically than have a man boss her around.

"But you're not healthy enough to take on the new alpha if he is anything close to Jeffery." She nodded and put the last dish in the china cabinet, then sat down as Grandmother took her hand and continued. "I'm very worried about you. You could have...you should have died that night."

"But I didn't. And we got away without much in the way of fines, too." Not any fines that any of them knew about, anyway. "I'm going to take the job. I've just decided. And you'll see, the alpha will fall all over himself when he gets a good look at all of us. We're a sexy bunch of women."

She wiggled her brows at her grandmother, which made her laugh. When Opal came in to say that the pizzas were there, she and her grandmother pulled out the paper plates and napkins as ten large pizzas loaded with meat and cheese were carried in. The pizza guy could hardly talk he was drooling so badly, and it wasn't because of the tantalizing smells coming from the boxes. Once he was on his way, they sat down to dig in.

"I think you could have not tipped him and he would have been thrilled." Jade reached for another slice as she continued. "I never seen anyone so overwhelmed by us as he was. You'd think he never saw a girl before."

Sapphire looked around the room, thinking about her earlier statement about them being sexy woman. They were, she supposed. All of them were tall, at well over five foot ten inches, thin as rails as her grandmother called them, but muscular and toned. Dark hair graced the head of each of them, and the dark brown eyes of their kind. They were all wolves, thanks to their heritage, and could withstand much more than humans could, as well as eat more as they burned a great deal more energy. She smiled at her grandmother when she commented on the state of their clothing.

"If a man walked in this house right now, he'd swear we're all a bunch of slobs. I never knew that moving could cause a person to get so nasty and messy," Grandmother said. Opal snorted. "And you, young lady, where on earth did you get that shirt? I think we should put it out to pasture."

They kidded around a great deal more as they finished off the last slice. Sapphire only hoped that once they were all settled in jobs and the house that they'd see this for what it was. A new start.

Her cell rang when she was putting the mattress on her bed. She started to answer it without looking, but decided at the last minute to look. She felt her wolf stir at the name that popped up. Jeffery was still trying to reach her. Letting it go to voicemail if he wanted to leave her a message, she started to fill the tub to take a long soak. Her room, like Jade's, had its own bathroom and huge tub.

An hour later she was wrapped in her favorite robe and sitting on the bed when she finally reached for the phone again. There were eight messages and ten missed calls. When she looked at her recent history, seven were calls from Jeffery, two from her aunt, and one unknown. She groaned when she realized she had to listen to all the messages before she knew who the unknown was.

Jeffery had left her the first three messages, and in each one he got a great deal nastier to her. Simply deleting them, she listened to her aunt going on about pack loyalty and rules on the next two. She was another reason they'd left so quickly. The woman was so deep in the pack that Sapphire always wondered why she wasn't the alpha. The next two were from Jeffery again, which she didn't even bother listening to before deleting. The last one was from someone at the office she was going to work at.

"Miss Erickson, this is Blair Henson from Flair Marketing. I was wondering if you could give me a call. I know it's sort of late, but I need to speak to you about an important matter concerning your working for my firm. There have been a few calls from a Jeffery Benetton." He left his phone number and ended the call.

"Fuck." Well, she supposed that this would have happened sooner or later. When her grandmother had notified the alpha here about them being in the area, he would have called Jeffery to find out all he could. It wouldn't have taken Jeffery long to figure out where she would work after getting the address of the new alpha, and he'd call there as well. She wished now she had listened to his messages. Then again, maybe not.

Tossing the phone to the bedside table, she didn't bother calling Mr. Henson back. What would be the point? Jeffery had fucked that up, and the man more than likely wanted to tell her to forget it. She would start looking for something else tomorrow. She added job hunting to her mental list and turned off the lights.

Tomorrow, she decided she was going for a long hard run and tried her best to forget everything else. She was rolling to her back when her phone rang again. When it shut off, she reached for it again and turned it to mute. Closing her eyes, she decided that in addition to everything else, she was going to have her number changed, too.

She didn't toss and turn as she normally did before finally falling to sleep. She knew she was tired beyond words, and her body, after the bath, was so relaxed. She yawned twice before she felt her body falling into restfulness. She only thought of the job twice before succumbing to sleep. Once to think she wished she had been able to meet the owner before Jeffery fucked it up for her, and then again when she thought of Mr. Henson's voice. There was something so warm about it that made her toes curl even then. She was definitely going to make use of the vibrator if a voice could make her wet. Smiling, sleep claimed her.

Chapter 2

"The number you have dialed has been disconnected or no longer in service. If you feel you've reached this number in error please—"

Blair slammed the phone down in the cradle and looked up when someone cleared their throat. His dad was not anyone he wanted to talk to right at the moment. But when he sat down, Blair simply waited.

"I take it she's not returning your calls." He nodded. "Wonder what changed her mind. You think she heard about you being the new alpha, or she heard you're a pain in the ass to work for?"

"I'm not a pain in the ass to most people. Just the stupid ones." He flushed when his dad laughed. "Okay, I'm a pain in the ass, but I'm a very wealthy pain in the ass and have made the people who work for me rich, too."

"If you think money is all the reason they stay here, then you're dumber than I gave you credit for." He glared at his dad only to have him laugh more. "You should also know that Jeffery Benetton called here again. That man has a real hard-on for that woman. What do you suppose she did to him?"

"Okay, I think I've said this to you before. Don't use the word *hard-on* in the offices. Someone could take offense and sue. Secondly, and more importantly, I'd prefer you never say any words like that to me again. I have no idea why you think it's funny to make me feel uncomfortable when you talk like that, but there you have it."

"It's what I live for." Blair looked at the doorway when his secretary, Justine Troy, walked in after a short knock. Before his dad could make a no doubt dirty comment, Blair spoke first.

"Any information on the Erickson woman yet?" She winked at his dad and sat down next to him across from his desk.

"She's purchased the house on Manor Hill. You know which one, the large mansion that you placed a bid on when you were looking at houses. She and her family live there, but so far the only person that has had any contact with them, other than the previous alpha, is a pizza delivery kid." She smiled as she continued. "I don't think he's going to be very helpful either. All he could tell me was 'wow' and also 'man.' I have no idea what that means in male terms, but I can only surmise that the women are pretty."

She handed him a file that he took and opened. There was nothing in it more than a copy of the deed to the house as well as the names of the residents. He looked up at her when he realized the names.

"They're all gems." She nodded at him. "And this odd ball out, I'm assuming she's their mother or something?"

Annabelle Erickson's name did not match the others. When Justine didn't answer him, he looked up at her. She and his dad were flirting again. Damn it all to hell and back. Blair said her name and she turned to look at him.

"Grandmother. She's their grandmother. According to what I could find, their mother died some time ago and the father died about a year later. The oldest girl, Sapphire, was about ten, and the sisters all one year younger than the next oldest. They've lived with her since their father died." Justine handed him another file. "This is the stuff you asked for about their old alpha. He's a piece of work, and it's no wonder they left. Sapphire Erickson fought him about two weeks before they moved here, and rumor has it, she was torn up pretty badly. Jeffery Benetton nearly killed her, and she didn't do so badly tearing him a new ass either. I have pictures of him. Someone at the clinic that he runs took them, and you owe me for paying for them."

He nodded, distracted by the photos. If this female did this much damage to an alpha, then he thought they'd have trouble. She wasn't projecting a very good picture of herself right now. But this didn't really seem like the girl he'd hired sight unseen either. Her previous boss, Bruce Maxwell, had told Blair that Ms. Erickson was a hell of an artist, and she could make a client so happy they could charge double their fee and anyone would have paid it.

"You'll be lucky to have her on your staff. And not worry so much about her needing one weekend a month off. Shit, if she had asked, I'd have given her every weekend off, but she said she needed the money more." Blair smiled, just realizing now why she needed the weekend off. Her other boss obviously didn't know what she was. But he did.

And it was all a moot point when he couldn't contact her. Blair stood up and reached for his jacket. If she wouldn't call him back, he'd simply go and see her. He was standing near the elevator when he realized his father was standing beside him.

"You're not going with me." His dad didn't say anything. "I mean it. I want this woman to work for me, not sue me because you can't keep your mouth shut."

His dad laughed. "What a way to talk about your poor old dad. You know that I'm only teasing the women who work for you. Hell, I think most of them enjoy it. You should try it sometime. A little romance with a woman might get you laid more than once a year."

"Dad, please." He stepped into the wide opening the elevator made for him. "Can you not just let me do this? I know what I'm doing. I've been running this business for a long time."

"And a good job you're doing, too, but you need to stop working so dammed much and have some fun. You remember what that means, don't you? Going out with friends and buddies, getting naked with a woman?" Blair didn't comment, and that only seemed to encourage his dad more. "You do know that if you don't use it, it'll fall off. Then where will your mate be?"

"A mate is the last thing I need, thanks. And when I do need one, I'll make sure she doesn't care that I don't have time for sex." His dad snorted again. "You should also know that I've a good mind to get myself fixed. I really don't care for kids either."

That shut him up. His dad was still standing there in the yawning elevator when the doors shut. Blair was still laughing as he left the building. He'd have to remember that threat when he wanted to get the better of his dad. He'd never do that, but it was a nice threat all the same.

He drove himself to the address. He really didn't mind the limo when he was busy with paperwork in the back of it, but he also enjoyed a nice drive. And the drive out to the house was a pleasant one. When he pulled into the drive, he looked at the house that he'd wanted but could never convince the man who owned it to sell. He wondered why the man had sold it now and not contacted him like he'd begged him to.

Blair got out of the car and left his jacket inside. It was a warm day, yet he could feel the difference in the air around him here as opposed to the heat in the city. There was a lot to be said for moving out into the country. He was just lifting his hand to knock when he was nearly bowled over by a flash of green and woman.

"Sorry, late for class. Go on in. Grandmother is in the kitchen. She's pissed, so tread carefully." The woman stopped and grinned at him as she continued. "You're not here to fix the fridge, aren't you?"

"No, I'm here to—" She waved again and got onto a big bike and took off. "That wasn't all that helpful."

He turned back to the door and heard someone cussing from deep within. When he shouted "hello" the woman told him to get his ass in there and stop screwing around. He moved toward the sound of the voice, wondering if the entire household was this rude.

The older woman standing in the middle of the huge kitchen looked on the verge of tears. He wanted to reach for her to comfort her, but was put off slightly by the large hammer she was holding like a weapon.

"It just stopped working. It couldn't have done this before I went to the grocery store. Oh no, it had to do it when I have all this food to fill it with." She looked at him. "You're not the repair man."

"No, ma'am, but I can have a look at it if you want." She nodded at him, but still held the hammer. "Do you think you could put that down? I'm not into having you miss whatever it was you were going to use that on and hitting me instead."

She tossed it in the general direction of the table and it rattled to the floor. There were nine full bags of food on it, as well as several on the counters and the floor near what he thought was a pantry. He pulled out his cell phone and called his butler and cook. Rocky answered on the first ring.

"What do you know about refrigerator repair? I'm at a friend's house, and hers just died on her. And she's got a lot of groceries."

"Buy a new one." He looked around the room and wondered if there was time to get someone out to look at it or do as Rocky suggested.

"Can you do that for me? Have a big one brought out. I mean huge." Blair looked at the woman who was mumbling under her breath and putting things into the cabinet. "Make it fast, too."

When he gave him the address and hung up, the woman turned to him. She looked a good deal better than when he'd come in. And when she smiled at him for whatever reason, he felt he'd been given a gift.

"Most of the girls aren't here if you've come calling." He raised a brow at her, and she laughed. "What on earth would a good looking wolf like you want to come sniffing around an old woman and her problems like me for if not to see about her granddaughters?"

"I was trying to find your granddaughter—" The door opened and two of the most beautiful women he'd ever seen walked in. He grabbed the back of the chair that was nearest him. The one that had nearly knocked him over was very pretty from what he could see of her, but these women took his breath away.

"You're not the repair man." He shook his head at the first one that had come through the door. "Too bad. I'd like to watch you bend over the sink and have you unplug it."

"Diamond." The low warning had him looking at the other woman. "What do you want? If you're here about the meeting this moon, we've told the pack leader we're not interested. We informed him that we're in the area and that's all we have to do."

Blair would have to look into that, but for now he wanted to find the woman he'd come here for. He cleared his throat twice before he could speak, and flushed when the older woman laughed.

"I've come to see Sapphire Erickson. Are either of you her?" Diamond looked back at her sister, then at him. He just knew that this one was going to be her.

"If you're here because of Benetton, I'm not going back. And if you think you're man enough to try and make me, then I would suggest that you rethink that shit fast. I'm not a pushover. I've taken on men much bigger than you and walked away." Blair felt the need to move toward her...not just a need to be near her, but an overwhelming need to touch her, too. She took a step back, and he realized he'd moved.

"I'm Blair Henson. You were asked to call me back several times about working for me. If you found other employment, then the courteous thing to do would have been to call and let me know." He looked at Diamond when she laughed.

"Sapphire is neither courteous nor employed. She's been looking, but there doesn't seem to be a lot of...how shall I say, very well-mannered men around these parts to work for." He felt his wolf stir when Diamond continued. "The last guy asked her if she was good on her knees. It took my sister a full minute to understand what the fuck he meant by that."

He watched Sapphire pink up, and he had an image of her ass doing the same when he spanked her. Christ, he needed to get out of here, take his dad's advice, and get laid. When an Amazon of a woman like this one made his cock leap at the thought of dominating her, he was in serious trouble. Before he could move to the door and out into the cooler air than was currently in this kitchen, his phone rang.

"You there still?" His dad never greeted anyone when he had a point to make or a question to ask first. "I just got word from Rocky that he's bringing a fridge out to you. You thinking of moving in?"

"No." Blair took a deep breath when he realized how loudly he'd answered his father. "No, I'm just helping out. You're not coming, too, are you?"

"I'm in the truck now." His dad laughed. "I don't suppose you could introduce me to the woman who got you to buy her a fridge, do you? Might be someone I could lay claim to since we both know you won't."

The low growl of warning slipped past his lips before he could stop it. His dad didn't say anything for several seconds, and Blair was worried that he'd just opened a can of worms that his dad was going to enjoy teasing him with. But he didn't.

"You've met her, haven't you? One of them girls is your mate." Blair turned to Sapphire as what his dad was saying sunk in. "You can't hide the truth from me, son, if it's her, then you'll know it."

"It's not. I don't know what you're talking about." He closed his phone before his dad could say anything else. He looked at Sapphire, not sure what to do with her now.

"What do you want?" The first answer to her question popped into his head was *you*. But he doubted that she'd take that very well. "When I didn't call you back, I assumed you'd fill the position with someone else."

Every word that she said seemed to have a double meaning to him, and he couldn't speak past thinking of her in a few positions, one of which was across his lap naked. He wished now he had his jacket to hide his aching erection. He stepped more behind the chair.

When Diamond handed him a bottle of water, he nearly begged her to pour it over him. But he opened it and drained it. When she smiled at him, he had a feeling this sister was well aware of what was going through his head. He wasn't sure what to make of her when Sapphire spoke again.

"You never answered me. What do you want here?" He had to sit down. Nearly tumbling into the chair had her looking at him strangely, but right now he didn't give a good...he was not going to think of fucking right now, and nearly jumped out of his pants when he heard a car pulling into the drive.

"That'll be my dad and Rocky. They're bringing a refrigerator. I don't know how to fix this one." Before any of them could say a word, he was out the door and in the drive, just as his dad was getting out of the truck. His dad looked at him hard, and Blair was ready to bolt when he finally spoke.

"You all right, son?" He nodded and then shook his head. "Yeah, that's about right. Which one is she? The oldest?"

"This can't be happening right now." His dad only nodded at him. "Dad, I'm leaving here. Can you please tell them I had an emergency and I had to...Christ, I'm falling apart."

"That you are. Buck up, boy, you can't run from this. Go on in and introduce me to her." He looked over his shoulder, and Blair turned when he whistled. "Christ, son, you sure know how to pick 'em."

Sapphire stood alone on the porch with her arms crossed over her chest and looked down at them both. Blair's wolf snarled at him to go to her and to mark her, but he moved away. He felt him claw harder at his skin until he was ready to shift and claim her himself. Blair got into his car and started it with shaky hands. He was down the drive and onto the street before he let go of the breath he'd been holding.

"Mother fuck." Pulling over to the side of the road, he gulped in cool air-conditioned air as fast as it spilled from the vents. His entire body was on fire for him to shift and to claim the woman. He'd never had a reaction like this to a female in his entire life, and didn't care for it much right now. He sat there for ten minutes before he could move into traffic again.

He was nearly back to the office when his phone rang. He pressed the button to have the speaker turned on and was blasted by so much cursing he couldn't help but smile. When the woman—and for some reason he knew it was Sapphire—took a breath to no doubt start again, he interrupted her. He felt safe now that they had miles between them.

"I would think you'd have better luck getting a job if you cleaned up your mouth." Thoughts of her mouth had him reaching down to adjust his cock for the fiftieth time since he'd left her. And when she growled at him, he nearly had to pull over again and try to calm his body. Christ, she was going to kill him no matter the distance between them.

"Why is there a new refrigerator in my kitchen and your butler helping my mother put things in it? And what the fuck does your dad mean when he said I have a contract with you? I never said I'd work for you positively." But she had, and they both knew it. "I wouldn't work for a lunatic like you if you were the last place on earth to work."

He started to count to ten before he spoke, but thought, "fuck this shit" and let her have it. "You will work for me starting tomorrow or I'll have your pretty little ass in court for breach of contract so fast that your head will spin. And as for my dad, you'll be nice to him, or so help me I'll make your last alpha look like a walk in the park. And another thing you might want to think about is that as of three days ago, I'm the new alpha in this territory."

He pressed the end button just as she started to say something. He was pulling into his parking spot when he realized what he'd just done. He'd hired her to work for him when every part of his mind was screaming at him to keep her as far from him as he could possibly get her. He was still sitting there ten minutes later when his dad called him.

"You went and made this house a fan of yours. Never seen a bunch of more pissed off women in my life. I think maybe that Sapphire would gladly tear you to pieces and not have a second thought about it." His dad was probably right.

"I hired her." His dad said he knew that. "She's not my mate, but a woman who my wolf nor I, neither one, like very much."

"You don't believe that, do you?" His dad had asked him so softly that Blair wasn't sure it was his mind thinking it or him speaking, but his next words confirmed who had said it. "The woman isn't going to come any easier to you than you are to her. I'm thinking sparks are going to do

23

more than fly when you two get together. Christ, son, she's more than I ever hoped for in a daughter-in-law." His dad laughed, and Blair pulled the phone free and got out of his car to go to his office.

"I'm not taking her as my mate. I don't need her, and I certainly don't want her. And I would very much appreciate it if you never brought it up again." His dad laughed. "This isn't funny, Dad. You either drop it or I'll bar you from the building."

"I won't bring it up again, but if you think that's going to stop you from thinking about her every waking moment until you do something about her, then you've not been paying attention to me all these years. She's a done deal, and so are you."

Blair put his phone in his pocket without answering him but knew, just knew, that he was right. This thing between him and Sapphire was going to be there. He decided that he'd avoid her until his wolf finally figured out she wasn't his mate, too. Starting the first thing, he was going to be working well away from her. Forever if need be.

He was so fucked.

Chapter 3

She was in a vile mood, and Annabelle had a feeling it was because of the young man from yesterday. She'd never seen Sapphire take such a dislike for someone as she'd done him. And it was apparent that the young man was having the same reaction to her granddaughter. Annabelle looked up at the clock and cleared her throat.

"I'm going," Sapphire said, looking up from her breakfast. "I don't want to do this. I did sign a contract, but I didn't know he was going to be such a pigheaded prick. I don't want to work for someone like him."

"Hmmm, and he's the new alpha, too. I called one of the women that I met the other day, and she said that Blair was going to challenge the old alpha, but the man had a heart attack that night and died. He didn't look all that healthy when I was there, so it's no surprise to me." Sapphire continued to sit, and Annabelle decided enough was enough. "He's your mate, isn't he?"

"No." She shifted on her seat as she continued. "I don't want anything to do with him. Not now, not ever. I won't be saddled with a cold, heartless bastard. If I had wanted a man like that, I would have stayed back in our old pack and mated with Jeffery."

"But Jeffery was never going to be your mate." Sapphire stood up and moved to the door. "Honey, you can't run from this. Sooner or later the two of you are going to have to work this out."

"No, we won't. I'll just avoid him until he fires me. I'm pretty sure that might happen today, too." Annabelle didn't like the look on her face. "I might not have the job I want, but I'll do anything rather than work for him."

Annabelle watched her eldest granddaughter get into her truck and leave. She almost felt sorry for her. The poor thing, both of them actually, were in for a rude awakening if they actually thought they could keep apart. Annabelle wasn't sure why she believed that Blair would try the same thing as Sapphire and work to stay away from her, but it wouldn't work. They'd have to come together, sooner rather than later. Smiling, she turned to find Diamond staring at her.

"She's his mate, isn't she?" Annabelle nodded and started to load the dishwasher as she sat down. "I don't think they're going to be a match made in heaven, do you?"

"No. I think they'll be a hell of a match, but it's going to be a long, hard road before either of them realizes they can't win." Annabelle smiled and revised her statement. "I think they'll both win in the end, but the end is going to be a long way from easy."

"I think you're right. I don't think that Sapphire will ever forget what Jeffery did to her, and she'll have a hard time trusting anyone again." Annabelle had never really heard what had happened that night, only that Sapphire had been gravely injured, and Jeffery had banned them from the pack forever. Even now she didn't ask, because she wasn't sure she ever wanted to know.

After the others left, Annabelle went out to the garden. The tractor had shown up late last night to turn over the plot of ground, but it had been too dark to do much more than point to where she wanted a garden put. The man was supposed to come back this morning and finish the job for her. She had it all blocked off by the time he showed up. Two hours later, she was hoeing out a nice row.

"Nice place for a garden, I think." She turned to stare at the man from yesterday. She almost couldn't remember his name, but he smiled and told her. "Allen Henson. I'm Blair's father."

"I'm sorry. I wasn't aware that anyone said you were coming out." She usually wrote things like that down and felt bad that she hadn't remembered.

"I just showed up on my own. I was hoping to get to talk to you without the others around. About the kids." She nodded and moved to the end of the row when he picked up a hoe, too. "Don't stop on my account. I'll work with you so we can talk a bit. I've not done this sort of work in a while. I think I'll enjoy this."

She nodded, not sure what Sapphire would think about Blair's dad being there, but decided what she didn't know wouldn't hurt her. She watched the man move down the furrows with practiced ease and started on her own row as she spoke.

"She's his mate, as I'm sure you're aware." He said he was. "She doesn't want him and figures to get fired today so he'll break the contract with her. I don't think they realize that it won't do her a bit a good."

He laughed. "I'm thinking he'll try to do the same. And you're right, won't do them a lick of good. They're as good as mated now. Too bad really, that they won't listen to their elders. Sure would save them a great deal of time and heartache."

She didn't say anything as she finished her row and began another. Her granddaughter was ten kinds of stubborn. She'd gotten that from her grandda. She looked up when a cell phone went off and watched as Allen put it away without answering.

"My son. He's called me three times since I left the office. No doubt telling me that he's going to murder me again." Annabelle was shocked until he laughed. "He's just pissy because I set Sapphire up in the room next to his and had her trained by a less than competent employee. By the end of the day if those two aren't tangled on his desk, I'll be surprised."

"Sapphire isn't going to be easy. She's been hurt. Both physically and her heart. She's been hiding behind her shield of anger for a long time, and she's gotten really good at turning people away." Annabelle finished her row and waited for Allen so she could plant the tomatoes she'd bought. She looked up at him when he handed her a small spade. "Thank you."

"No problem. I saw them pictures of the alpha she beat to shit. What did he do to her?" Annabelle stopped in the middle of planting her first plant. There had been pictures? "I'm sorry, I thought you knew."

"No, I hadn't realized...were there any of my granddaughter?" Allen shook his head. "I only saw her afterwards, about a week afterwards. Diamond had nursed her back to health. I guess she was so injured that she couldn't even shift. I heard from Ruby, another granddaughter, that they'd thought that she was going to die."

"He didn't fare any better, I guess. She nearly castrated him from what the report said. And it's iffy whether or not he'll be able to get...have a...." He flushed, and she laughed. "Sorry about that. I usually just say what I'm thinking, and can't do that around you for some reason."

"It's because I'm old. You have to have respect for me." He shook his head. "If you say that I'm not old I won't believe another word that comes out of your mouth."

"No, it's not that. I think...I was thinking that we'd be related and that I didn't want to treat you like I do the others." He bent to plant the cabbage he had in his hand and spoke from there. "You have any ideas how to bring the two of them together sooner rather than when one or both of them hurts the other?"

"Leave them be." She put in the next two tomatoes before she said anything more. "If we push this, they'll work harder at not coming together. If we manipulate them, then it will come back to bite us in the ass."

"You sound as if you know this for a fact."

She nodded and realized he couldn't see her. "I do. My parents did the same with my mate and me. I fought very hard not to be with him, and in the end...." She shrugged. "I loved him after a fashion, I suppose, but not the kind that we might have had. My son loved his mate. Gave her six daughters and never cared at all they never had a son. He was as happy with them as he'd ever been. His little gems, he called them from the day they were born. Then their mother died and.... Well, I don't think he ever got over it."

They finished the garden together just talking about the girls and the garden she was hoping to expand next season. When he left her an hour later, she went in to check on the roast she had in the oven and thought about her granddaughters.

She loved them dearly. She always would, but she didn't care for this mating business and the way it made a couple want so desperately, and for what? She had lied to Allen; she'd never loved her husband, but he'd given her a son, and for that she'd forever be grateful to him. She only hoped that Sapphire would have the same someday, if not a great love as her father had had.

~~~

"I don't know." Sapphire looked at the man and wanted to strangle him. He'd been in here with her since she'd arrived, and she was no closer to knowing what her job was than when she'd come in the door. He looked around the room as if the answer to her question, a very simple question, she thought, would suddenly appear for him.

"Look. It's on your website. Just go there and see who your biggest clients are. What is it you do here again?" He grinned at her, and she felt the hair on the back of her neck stand up. He was creepy, too.

"Maybe if we were under a different setting I wouldn't be so nervous." She mentally rolled her eyes at him as he continued. "Why don't we go and have a drink somewhere and I could tell you all about this job."

"Because it's only ten-thirty in the morning. Where is your boss?" He moved his finger down her arm, and she stood up. "Touch me again and I'll tear your throat out."

His laughter had her wolf stir, but either he was too stupid to notice or he simply didn't care she moved back when he reached for her again. He was both, she decided in that minute, and took his hand when he moved to touch her breast.

When the door opened behind her, she didn't bother turning. The man she had on the floor with his hand bent back just before the breaking point had her full attention.

Laughter told her it was a female that had come in, and when a male cleared his throat, she spoke. There was no way they'd keep her after this.

"He touched me when I asked him several times and in two different languages not to. And this time, when he reached for my tit, I'd had enough. If this is this company's idea of making their employees happy, I'm not sure we're going to mesh."

"He touched you?" Sapphire jerked around to see Blair standing there and the woman who had shown her in here holding him back. "He fucking touched her."

"I heard her. Calm him or there will be hell to pay." Miss Troy looked over at her and the guy she had on the floor. "Can you please step away from that idiot before his animal comes out and tears him apart?"

Sapphire let go of the man, and he stood and hit her before she could move away. She knew that she hit him back, but she was knocked out of the way almost as soon as he hit the floor. The pain in her head exploded, and she felt her wound at her back tear open again. Blackness didn't just come over her but stormed through her like a tornado going across the flatlands. She woke in a dark office lying on a couch, and sat up slowly.

"Do you still hurt?" She didn't answer Blair but moved to stand up. "I asked you a question, and I'd very much like an answer."

"I fucking hurt. Is that what you wanted to hear? What the hell hit me?" She staggered slightly and moved back when he was suddenly in front of her. "Don't touch me, please. I hurt in too many places to name right now."

"I'm sorry. I didn't...you should have backed away when you were told." She didn't bother telling him she had it under control but went to the door and hopefully freedom from him. "Who cut you up like that? Jeffery?"

"He and I had a little disagreement, and we both walked away with a few cuts and bruises." Blair laughed a short bark of laughter that made her think he didn't think it was the least bit funny.

She put her hand on the doorknob when she felt his breath on her neck. "You smell like nothing I've ever smelled before."

Sapphire opened the door and had to press her body against his to get it to open enough for her to walk out. He moaned at her, and she nearly leaned back into him. But she was leaving this loony bin and not returning. Blair put his hand over hers when she went to press the elevator button.

"I've fired Dan. I should have killed him, but Justine thought it would be too hard to explain. You should have found me when he touched you." She turned to him as she jerked her hand from under his. "I won't tolerate you doing this sort of playing here again."

"Really?" He nodded. "Well, good for you. I nearly get raped by one of your employees and it's entirely my fault. And would you have cared very much if I had touched him in the same manner? Would he have been knocked on his ass and me fired?"

"He should know better, and so should you. I won't have men touching you." She pressed the down button before he could stop her. "You're not going anywhere, Miss Erickson. We have to discuss your behavior while you work in this office."

She laughed at him and turned when the doors opened. She stepped in the opening and pressed the button to go down without speaking to him. She had a feeling that when she got to the lower floors there was going to be someone waiting for her to escort her back up, but she wasn't going to give him the satisfaction. Pressing all the numbers, she got off at the next floor down, went to the staircase, and went up and not down. When she was on the roof, she looked around at all the buildings surrounding his and saw that if she got a good enough run at it, she could leap to the next building and leave from there.

It was stupid move, she knew that. With as much pain as she was in and how much her head hurt right now, she should just simply go down and let someone take her home. But not now, not after the way he'd treated her. The man was going down, and she was going to laugh her ass off when he fell. If, and that was looking like a big if, she didn't fall first.

Tossing her purse to the other building, she took off her heels and tossed them over as well. When she felt she could do it, she went to the other side of the building and breathed deeply several times before she took off running. When the building was there for her to jump to, she had second thoughts, and that was all it took for her to stumble slightly. She caught her leg on the last step and nearly fell to her death when she touched the other side with her hands.

It took her three tries to heave her body up onto the other roof. And when she did, she lay there for several minutes just trying to slow her pounding heart. When she sat up, she reached for her first shoe and decided that she was entirely too unsteady for walking on them, and limped her way to the other one and her purse. When she was at street level she hailed a cab, glad now that she'd parked on the next street over. She lay in the back, resting when the cab started moving.

She wasn't going back there. He was too demanding for them to ever get along, and he lived in another decade...even if it was just as her working for him as an employee. She'd never make it as his mate, and she certainly didn't want to.

By the time she drove home, she was hurting so badly that she was sure she'd never be able to get out of the car, much less up to her room. She saw the two cars in the drive but didn't care to socialize just then, and went around to the back of the house and in the kitchen.

Her grandmother was pouring tea when she opened the door. Before she could say anything her grandmother put her finger to her lips and shook her head. Then in a loud voice she called to the other room.

"I just checked my phone, Mr. Henson, and I've no messages from her as yet. You say she left your office and you didn't see her leave? How strange." Grandmother pointed to the back stairs, then picked up the tray and headed out. "Do you think she's still in the building then?"

"No. I don't know what happened to her, but she's not in the building. I had security go over every inch of it." Sapphire moved to the back stairs and slowly made her way up. She wished she could have stayed and listened to whatever else Blair had to say about his search for her, but the door had closed and she wasn't in the mood to listen at doorways. She met Diamond coming down the stairs, and she helped her the rest of the way up to her room.

"Blair is downstairs." Sapphire nodded at her sister. "I figured you knew. I think Grandmother is having fun at his expense. I let her know that you'd called me so she would know what do to. How did you know he'd come here?"

Sapphire had called Diamond when she'd gotten to her car to ask her to tell grandmother she was running late. She also told them to expect Blair, and he'd be spitting mad.

"Because he doesn't like to lose." She took off her blouse and left her bra and panties on. She was hurting too much to take them off, and after Diamond made sure she wasn't going to die by morning from her old and recent wounds, she closed her eyes. She'd have to avoid him for the next few days if she wanted to be able to heal after all this.

"Sapphire, what would it hurt to have him as your mate? I mean, wouldn't he protect you from Jeffery when he comes here? We both know that he's going to. He doesn't like to lose, either."

She knew her sister was right, but she didn't have the energy to talk to her tonight. She certainly didn't have the strength to explain to her that he didn't want her as much as she didn't want him. And the pain around her heart had nothing to do with him or his rejection of her.

Chapter 4

Blair sat at his desk for over an hour, trying not to think of Sapphire. He'd never been more frustrated with a woman in his life. Actually, he'd never been more frustrated with anyone in his life as he was with her. She'd run from him, and he was still trying to figure out how the hell she'd done it and why he gave a shit. His phone ringing made him glare at it.

"There's a Miss Erickson here to see you." His heart took a strange leap before Justine clarified. "Diamond Erickson."

He wanted to tell her to tell the woman to fuck off, but needed...no, that wasn't right. He was curious to know where Sapphire was. When he told Justine to send her in, he stood up and came around to the front of his desk to greet her.

"Good morning, Diamond. And to what do I owe this pleasure—?"

"Don't fuck with me and I won't you." He started to snap at her, but he simply nodded and sat down. "I'm here about my sister. She's hurt, did you know that?"

"I hurt her yesterday when I moved her away from...." Diamond was shaking her head. "Then I don't understand. How else was she hurt? If you're talking about the wound on her back, I didn't cause that one."

"Jeffery Benetton did that and a great deal more to her. And yesterday trying to get away from you, she hurt herself even more. She had a broken rib and a gash on her left hip that I had to put fifteen stitches in after she went to sleep." Diamond sat down across from him as she continued. "Did you know that she gave up everything to keep us safe from men like you?"

"I'm nothing like Benetton, and I resent you coupling my name with his." She only stared at him, and he shifted on his seat. "Why are you here?"

"I came to see what kind of man you are. I'm not impressed." She stood up, and he thought she was going to leave, but she only started pacing. "Jeffery put us up for auction. He had us pulled from our beds and chained together like animals. We couldn't shift or the chains around our necks would have killed us. Then he cut our clothes from us and paraded us around the pack meeting place to show our wears, as he called them. Sapphire was the only one not with us. She...she'd been taken away so he could do it."

"But she came back." Diamond nodded. "What happened to her that had her sent away?"

"She'd been shot. Three times and taken away from us. We thought he'd killed her, but he'd only pissed her off." She turned to him then. "You've never seen her pissed. Her wolf is nothing like you've ever seen before, and when they're both there...." She shivered.

"Is this the night that they fought?" She nodded again. "Why didn't anyone help you? It's against pack law for him to treat single females like that. Especially ones in a pack where there are few women and little in the way of new pack coming to them."

"Do you really think he gave a shit what the laws are? He was pissed off at Sapphire because she wouldn't have him in her bed, and he was going to make us all pay." She took an envelope from her shirt and handed it to him. "The decree he had us all sign before any of this happened. He had us all tied up in neat little bows, and we couldn't do a damned thing about it."

He read over the first page before looking up at her. "It says here that he can break in any female he wishes before she goes to her mate. No matter what the age."

"He said it was his right as alpha. If you look at the signatures, you'll see that none of us signed out names. That was Sapphire's idea. She said that no matter what, we were to never sign anything coming from him. That included." He laughed when he read the names they'd scrawled across the document. He'd bet anything that Sadie Earholder was Sapphire.

"When we were being shown off Grandmother was tied to a tree. They'd stripped her down as well and blindfolded her. Anyone walking by her could and did grab at her. I think that was what sent Sapphire over the edge." She started pacing again as she continued and Blair had a feeling she was no longer in the room with him but back in the field.

"She killed three men before anyone knew she was there. I watched her take out one of them but said nothing to the others. I didn't want them to give her away. When the fourth man suddenly disappeared, I knew that it was only a matter of time before she went after Jeffery. He was just taking off his pants to rape…to rape me when she attacked him." She looked out the window as the rain streamed down the glass. "She never gave him the chance to shift before she tore at him. Blood splattered over us as she tried to kill him. Two of his men attacked her then, and another tried to use me as a shield. It wasn't until his head landed at my feet that I realized that she'd killed him. His body dropped from mine just as I heard her scream. I took the keys from the dead man and unlocked the others and took them to safety. Grandmother was bleeding pretty badly by then, but it was mostly from the sticks they'd used and not the other wolves."

"His wounds that he inflicted on her won't heal. That's why she still hurts so much." Diamond nodded at him. "I forgot about that until just now. Until she takes a mate, or another alpha seals the wounds, she'll never heal. It's a sign that the male of her pack has hurt her."

"He'll come for her. I'm surprised that he's not been here already. He, like you, won't simply give up." He wanted to tell her he wasn't like the other alpha again, but in this he knew she was correct. "When he gets here, she'll die. And it will be partly your fault."

He wanted to deny it, wanted to tell her she was wrong, but he knew she wasn't. He looked up at her as she stood staring out the window and thought she'd come here more than just to tell him what a fucking bastard he was, but for something else.

"What do you want me to do? Back off? I'm trying to do that, but you should know that I'm having a hard time doing that. I don't want her. She'll never fit into the mold I have in my mind for a mate, and I like my life the way it is. And she and I would never suit as a couple." He didn't tell her that all he wanted from her was a quick lay and he'd be satisfied. He wasn't even sure that would work anymore.

No matter how many times he jerked off, he still wanted to find her and take her hard against the closest hard surface he could find.

Diamond nodded and moved to the door without answering him. He started to go after her to…he wasn't sure what, but he knew she'd washed her hands of him. When she was at the door, she stopped and turned to look at him once more.

"He'll kill her when he comes. I'm not telling you this to make you do anything you don't want. I'm telling you so that when it happens, and it will, you'll know that we'll leave here and never darken your door again. We'll…we'll move on as you will now. And I promise you, as much as I'd like to believe otherwise, no one will ever blame you."

She was gone for a full five minutes before he could move. Diamond had found him lacking. He had no idea why that hurt so much, but it did. He moved to Justine's desk and barely saw her until she was standing in front of him.

"What's happened?" Blair stared at her until she hit him in the face. "Snap out of it and tell me what's happened to Sapphire? Is she hurt? And if so, how badly?"

He looked around his offices and at the furniture he'd paid entirely too much for simply because it had been the first thing he'd been shown by the decorator. At the art on the wall that he rarely looked at because he thought it was the ugliest shit he'd ever seen. Then he looked at Justine.

"I'm a failure." She started to speak, but he stopped her. "I am. I might be wealthy and have everything I've ever wanted, but as a human being or a wolf for that matter, I fucking suck." When she didn't disagree with him he felt worse. "I'm so sorry."

"What did she tell you that made you like this?" Justine sat on the edge of her desk, and he sat in the chair across from her. "Something must have happened in there. She comes out crying like you've taken her best friend from her, and you have an epiphany about what sort of person you are, or not for that matter."

"She basically told me that her sister had been abused enough that I should back the fuck away from her and let Benetton kill her when he comes for her. And she thinks this because she found me lacking as a person." He didn't wait for her to comment but went on. "And she's right. I am lacking as a person. I'm not involved in anyone's life. Not even my own. I have no patience for my dad when he comes here to talk to me, and I work entirely too much. And for what? More money? I have more now that I can spend in my lifetime even if I never work again. Prestige? Fuck that shit. I never wanted that anyway. Respect? I don't even respect myself, why would I expect anyone else to do the same to me?"

"Are you going to do anything with this newfound knowledge?" He looked at her, suddenly at a loss for an answer. "You have a mate now. Do you want her or not? Do you care if she dies or not? Do you want to give her up or fight for her?"

"She'll not be happy about any of this." Justine snorted. "She's going to be highly pissed at me and shove me away at every opportunity she gets."

"No doubt she will, but you still didn't answer my questions. What are you going to do now?" She stood up when he did. "There's a nice flower shop on the way...no, that'll never do with her. She's not the flowers and candy sort. She's more of a—"

"Loaded gun type?" He laughed when she nodded. "I'm not going to give her a gun even if I'm sure it's not loaded. This is going to have to be slow and easy."

He was out the door and in his car going to her house before he realized it. Blair decided that he was going to give Justine a raise. That was if he lived long enough to give it to her. He was sort of going into the lion's den here, and he had no way of knowing if he was going to survive it or not.

~~~

Jeffery moved much slower nowadays. The wounds Sapphire had inflicted on him were not healing as well or as quickly as he'd hoped. But it was his cock that caused him the most pain. He couldn't even piss out of it without enough pain to bring him to his knees.

The first time he'd taken a piss he'd ended up kneeling in his own urine, sobbing like a baby. He'd tried to crawl out of the mire, but he'd hurt so badly that he'd had to have someone come and get him. He'd had the man killed when he'd laughed at him. No one had laughed since.

He knocked on the front door of her house and waited for someone, anyone to let him in. The old broad opened the door. Before he could reach for the screen to enter, she had a gun pointed at him.

"That's far enough. What do you want?" He glared at her, trying to intimidate her, but she only laughed. "We don't belong to you any longer, Benetton, so can that crap now."

"I'm here to collect Sapphire. She's to stand trial for the injuries she caused her alpha." He'd had to call in a great many favors to get this thing going, and he was glad now that he'd had to give up so much for her arrest. "I'm here as a courtesy and to take her back with me."

"You've got to be kidding me. What about the injuries you caused her? Or the ones you caused to us? Are you going to be punished for any of that?" He thought that he'd paid dearly for their injuries, but said nothing as he reached for the screen again. "You touch that door again and I will blow what little of your dick is left off you."

His hand snapped back so fast that he hurt himself when his hand hit his ribs. He'd been surprised when he'd not healed right away, but his doctor, his own personal one, had told him it was because Sapphire was an alpha bitch. He knew that she was an alpha and hadn't realized the law about injury to another one of his kind and the problems it caused. He had wanted her simply to rip her throat out before she figured out she was a good deal stronger than he'd ever be.

Jeffery was just reaching for the door again to teach the bitch a lesson when one of the others, he thought it was Opal, stepped up behind her grandmother. He knew he could make her do what he wanted if for no other reason than he'd scared her badly before.

"Open this fucking door and let me in." She took a step back, then another. "You fucking heard me, cunt. Open this goddamned door now." When Sapphire was suddenly in front of him, he started for the door again. Then someone wrapped their arm around his throat, and he could only manage a strangled cry when the man spoke.

"You talk to her like that again and I will personally see to it that you never speak again." He felt the arm tighten as the man sniffed him. "I have your scent now, and if I find you in my territory again, I will do just what I said."

He was tossed against the wall beside the door as the man held him there with a large hand to his back. Jeffery would have struggled, but it was all he could do not to whimper and beg the man to let him go.

"You hurt?" Jeffery started to tell him he fucking was, but realized he wasn't talking to him. "Did he touch any of you?"

"No. He wasn't going to either. But I gotta admit I'm damned glad to see you." He glared at Annabelle as she went on about how happy she was that he'd shown up.

"I'm going to deposit him in his car. Do you think that when I get back we can sit down and talk? All of us?" Seconds later he was being turned around and pressed against the wall again. He got a good look at the man who would dare attack him.

"You'll pay for this." He nodded. "Do you have any idea who I am? What I am to these women and you? Alpha, you dumb motherfucker and—"

His head hit the wall three times as stars danced around his vision. Before he could say another word he was picked up and thrown off the porch and near the limo he'd come in. The driver didn't move when the man from the porch barked at him to stand down, and Jeffery found himself being lifted again and thrown in the back seat. The man loomed in the open door as Jeffery curled into a fetal position, the pain was so great.

"I'm Blair Henson, and this is *my* territory, you fucking prick. You come near what is mine again and I'll do more to you than Sapphire ever did. And this time you won't live through it. I'll make sure of it." He stood up, and Jeffery finally got his tongue back.

"She's supposed to come back with me to stand trial. She injured her alpha, and that's against all pack laws." The door slammed shut, and before he could get to the door and open it again, the car was moving. And from the way he was being thrown around he would say they were going pretty fast.

He was bleeding again by the time he was back to his hotel. He wasn't sure what the staff thought about him coming in all bent over and bleeding, but at this point he not only didn't care but almost wanted someone to put him out of his misery. Christ, he was sick of this shit.

Lying down on the bed, he tried to work through the pain his body seemed riddled with. His head was pounding so badly that he had to get up and close the curtains against the waning light. He wanted to take something for it, anything, but knew that it wouldn't work. His kind and drugs didn't work all that well. He reached for the pillow and pulled it over his eyes just as the phone rang.

"You should know that I've had enough of your bullshit and am taking steps to have you removed as alpha." His skin seemed to tighten around his body and his wolf curled away from him as Henson spoke. "If you come to my territory again, I will take measures to not only have you removed but end your very existence as well. Do I make myself perfectly clear?"

"Yes. But she's mine to do with as I please. Even you have to see that." The man laughed, a cold laugh that made Jeffery think of nails going down chalkboards and cats calling out in the dark, full of terror of unknown forces.

"She's mine."

The line went dead, and he lay there. Jeffery hated this feeling that ran through his body and the woman who had caused it. He had no doubt that this was all Sapphire's fault. And he knew that she was sleeping with the big wolf, too. Why else would he go to such unnecessary extremes if that wasn't the case?

Jeffery had wanted to kill Sapphire the moment he'd seen her. Her grace had been evident even when she was a young cub, and when she grew into her long coltish legs, and muscles began to take the place of baby fat, he'd nearly taken her when she'd came to the first pack meeting just after her change. Christ, he doubted there was ever a more beautiful woman. Then he'd figured out what she was and how fucking strong she was. He doubted that she ever knew what she was.

But she'd hated him from the start. Not only that, but had gone out of her way to piss him off every chance she got, starting with her refusal to have anything to do with him sexually, and that just wasn't right in his books. He'd had women wanting him since he was ten, and she had no right to refuse him anything. He was alpha.

His wolf seemed to agree with him and snarled at him. He didn't even bother trying to calm him because he loved his other self. Being a wolf was the greatest thing that could happen to a man, and if it wasn't for the fact that he needed females to breed, he'd get rid of all of them and simply fuck humans.

But Sapphire was going to be his or else. And she was going to pay for what she'd done to him. Not only for the wounds she'd given him, but for the embarrassment and humiliation he'd had to endure. Sapphire Erickson was going to pay dearly.

Chapter 5

Blair wasn't sure what he was supposed to do now. He'd never spent a great deal of time with the fairer sex, especially in a houseful of them. But he needed to get this thing worked out with Sapphire, and he had to figure out what the fuck was the other alpha's obsession with her...other than her obvious beauty.

Blair stood up when three of the women entered the living room and continued standing until they sat. When the elder woman came in, he stood as well and heard one of the women laugh.

"You're going to be exhausted by the time you leave if you continue to act like a jack in the box." Blair wasn't sure what to say to her, unused to people making fun of him. "I'm Opal, by the way. And these are my sisters Ruby and Emerald. And this lovely lady is our grandmother, Annabelle."

He nodded to each of them and looked at the door when two more sisters entered. There wasn't any doubt they were sisters, either. Each of them looked like the other. Dark hair, the same dark eyes, and a loveliness about them that made him think of queens. He was introduced to Jade and

Diamond, and then they sat down. There was no sign of Sapphire.

"She's…not coming." Blair looked at Diamond, who made it sound as if she knew why her sister wasn't coming down and blamed him.

"Why not?" Her shrug was no help at all. "I would like to speak to all of you, but mainly her. She's…you may as well know that she's my mate. I can't have her running around like she's—"

Diamond cleared her throat, and he had to think what he'd said. He was being arrogant again, he thought she was telling him, but he didn't know how to be anything else. He tried to think what to do when he thought of his dad. He would know just how to charm them. He reached for him now.

I'm lost. His dad laughed. *I mean I have six women here, and the one that I really want to talk to is not coming down to speak to me. What do I do?*

Why not go up and get her? Or better yet…this is Sapphire, right? Your mate? He told his dad it was. *Then get up to where she is and either charm her…no wait, you have no idea how to charm a woman. Just go up and take her to bed.*

Thoughts of her in his bed entered his mind and he had to close his eyes. Christ, she was driving him crazy. He'd had an idea last night that if he fucked her once and used protection he'd be over her. He had convinced himself that she was simply someone that didn't want him, so he'd manifested this idea that she was his mate. Then he woke up with a raging hard-on, and no amount of masturbating was helping. He was so fucked.

"Where is her room?" Annabelle drew in a sharp breath when he asked. "I'm not going to hurt her, but I do need to talk to her. This thing with the other alpha isn't going away, and I'd like to talk to her." He was babbling. He tried to look innocent, but he was pretty sure he was failing at that miserably. They were looking at him like he had three heads. Maybe he did. He certainly felt like it.

"Fourth floor to your right at the top of the stairs." He looked at Emerald. "You tell her I told you and I'll hunt you down and tear what I'm sure is an impressive dick off of you and serve it to the cats."

He was moving up the second flight when he thought about how violent these women were. All of them, and he was willing to bet that Annabelle would hold her own as well. When he rounded the stairs to go to the fourth floor, he looked down the spiral staircase. It was beautiful and well maintained, as was the rest of the house. He went to his right at the top of the stairs and knocked once. The faint "come in" had him taking a deep breath and opening the door.

Blair had no idea what he was going to say or if he had anything to say. She stood there in front of him in nothing more than towel wrapped around her like a toga and her hair gloriously hanging down around her shoulders.

"I didn't know it was you." He nodded at her as he took a step toward her. When she didn't move, he took a few more. The closer he got to her the more of her he wanted to see.

Brushing his hand over her shoulder, he pushed her damp hair out of his way. She moaned when he pressed his mouth against her warm skin. He wanted to bite her, mark her, and his wolf was snarling at him to do so, but he wouldn't. He didn't want her as his mate.

"You wanted to see me?" He moaned at her question and lifted his head to look down at her. He put his finger into the top of her towel where her breasts were spilling out of the top. Watching her eyes, he pulled it free from her.

"All of you." His breath whooshed out of him when she was bared to him. There were cuts and tears in her skin, some of them deep, others just scrapes. He saw claw marks that hadn't healed and bruises that were dark and ugly. But what he saw was perfection; it was what she was, simply perfection.

Cupping her breast, he ran his thumb over her hardened nipple and leaned down to take her mouth. She tasted of warmth and sex, and when her tongue brushed along his, he pulled her closer with his free hand.

"I want you." She nodded, and he picked her up in his hands, filling them with toned muscles and heat. As her legs wrapped around his waist, he moved to the big bed, happy that she didn't have one of those tiny little twins. As soon as her back touched the bed, he took her nipple in his mouth and suckled hard at it. Her scent hit him, and his cock hurt from the sudden tightness in his pants.

But he knew that taking her like this would mark her. And as much as he wanted to bury himself to the hilt in her, he couldn't...wouldn't do it. Moving down her body, nipping and licking a path to her navel, he swirled his tongue in the deep indentation and then moved down her body more. He was going to taste her and drink from her if it was the last thing he ever did.

Sitting up on his knees, he spread her legs open and laid them on either side of him. She sat up on her elbows, and he cupped his cock. This was only going to work if he didn't free himself like he so desperately wanted to do. Touching the wet curls at her apex, he slid into her and felt her tightness grip him, and he watched her body ride him.

"I'm going to taste you." She moaned and shook her head. He moved in and out of her quicker, wanting to watch her when she reached her release. "Come for me, Sapphire. I want to see you in the throes of passion. Then I want to drink from you as you fill me."

Blair pressed his thumb over her clit. She cried out but didn't come, surprise evident on her face. He had a thought that she was still a virgin, but found that idea rather silly. No woman as beautiful and as responsive as her would have made it much past high school intact. Using his thumb hard against her nubbin, he waited for her to come, and when she did, he nearly did take her then. Nothing could have prepared him for the way her climax affected him.

Moving back to bury his mouth over her, he nearly leapt onto her when she lifted her knees up and touched her clit with her own hand. She spread her lips open for him, and he dove in like a man starved. And when he got his first taste of her, he realized that he was indeed hungry for her.

He wasn't able to drink from her fast enough. Her juices poured from her body and into his mouth and onto the spread beneath them. Sucking at her, lapping at her, he swallowed her into him and knew that he'd never get enough. That if he took her now it would only be the beginning and he'd never get enough of her or her body. When she came again, screaming out his name, he pressed his finger into her, curling it until he found the spot that made her moan for him, made her dance over his mouth. Stretching her, filling her, he realized this wasn't enough, but he knew that taking more was out of the question.

Christ, Blair had never in his life wanted to fuck a woman like he did her. Lifting his head, he looked at her heaving breasts, hips moving up and down like a dance he wanted to enjoy with her. Reaching to his cock, he stroked it hard and knew that much more and he'd be coming in his pants. Taking her clit into his mouth again, he nipped hard and had her screaming again, begging him over and over to stop and to give her more. When he slid his fingers along her gate to her tiny puckered rosette, he felt her need, and he didn't try to be gentle, but pressed his thumb deep and felt her come apart again.

When she went limp on the bed, he sat up. She was beautifully sated and sleeping. He stood up, went to her bathroom, opened his pants, and freed his cock. He ran his hand down the length of himself and felt his balls tighten even more against his body. Fisting his cock hard, he thought of the taste of her juices, and he came with a shout, spilling his seed in his hand and watching as it shot out and over the counter. He was leaning against it when he heard her and turned to look at her.

"I'm sorry. I didn't mean to…." She looked back at the bed, then at him. "You could have had me. I would have…we could have…you could have done that inside of me."

He wasn't sure what to say that wouldn't come out all wrong, so he said what first popped into his head. "You should get some clothes on. Being naked around you is hard on me."

He hurt her. He knew it the moment the words spilled from his mouth. But she was gone before he could say he was sorry. Putting himself back together, he cleaned up the mess he'd made and went into the bedroom to talk to her. The room was empty. And when he looked, he noticed that her bed had been stripped clean of all evidence of what they'd just done. And for some reason that pissed him off. He went to find her.

~~~

Sapphire was stuffing all her linens in the washer when her grandmother walked in. She didn't say anything, but pulled the sheets out and put them on the floor and then put the comforter in. She was turning on the washer when Sapphire decided she would never sleep on them again and went to find a trash bag. *He* walked in when she was tying off the bag.

"What the hell is wrong with you?" She didn't answer him but dumped the bag on the floor next to the trash can. He picked it up, tore it open, and spilled the contents onto the floor. "You think this will somehow erase what we did up there?"

"You mean what *you* did. I did nothing but lay there." She knew she was lying but right now didn't care. "You hated what you did so much that you went to the bathroom and jerked off instead of taking what I was offering freely. Well, you missed your chance, big boy. I'll never spread my legs for you again."

He was furious, and she was pretty sure she'd pushed him just a little too far. But he snarled at her and she lost her temper. Reaching out, she slammed her fist into his face, and when he started to fall backwards, she put out her foot and hit him in the chest to finish the job. He hit the table so hard that it shattered under his weight. Blood pooled under his head as she stepped over him and out of the house. Shifting quickly, tearing her clothes in the process, she headed for the woods and didn't look back when her grandmother yelled at her.

Running as hard as she could, she let her wolf take her wherever she wanted. She didn't see anything as it blurred by her, only the occasional rock or a fallen log. She was near the large waterfall when she saw the deer. Not wanting to scare it, she moved to the water and dove in as she shifted to herself. Climbing the large stone wall behind the water, she sat on the very edge and looked out at the crystal clear water.

"What have I done?" Her voice echoed around her and came back. Letting the tears fall, she sat there and tried her best to think of nothing but the water in front of her and the stone at her back. But it did little good to try and forget what had happened.

They'd had sex. Well, she supposed that they really hadn't, but she'd enjoyed it. Very much so. He'd made her feel...something she'd not done in a very long time. Then when she'd heard him in the bathroom, she'd walked in to see him coming.

It had been beautiful and had left her speechless. When he'd turned to look at her, she wasn't sure what to say. Her first thought had been to ask him if she could taste him as he had her, but she'd seen the anger in his face, seen that he'd been caught at something that he'd probably prefer she didn't see. And she was hurt when he told her that her body was sickening to him. She looked down at the wounds and realized they probably were. She brought her knees up to her chin and let the water wash away the tears.

Sapphire knew that she was pretty. Not beautiful like her sister Diamond, and she wasn't cute like Emerald was. Men loved them for what they were. She had been nothing men had wanted. Except for Jeffery.

He'd never made her feel the things that Blair did. From the first moment she'd seen him, she had wanted to touch him. But Jeffery had made her feel dirty, like she needed a hot shower afterwards and enough detergent to get her body raw with it. She supposed that was how she felt now.

She had no idea how long she sat there. She heard her name a couple of times. Once had been Blair, and she heard him cursing at her. Then her sister. She wasn't sure which one, but she'd bet it was Ruby. Diamond would just leave her alone, so she knew it wasn't her. When she stood up to dive into the water to leave, she noticed that it had gotten dark, and as she swam to the shoreline, she could see that the nocturnal animals had come out and were feeding. Shifting to wolf, she quietly made her way back to the house, but reached for Diamond before coming into view of the house.

Is he gone? She laughed, and Sapphire wanted to go back out to the falls and live there the rest of her life, but Diamond finally answered.

Oh, he's gone all right, but has left strict orders for us to call him the moment we see you. I'd very much appreciate it if you didn't make me have to call him and stay out of sight. I'll go down and leave you clothes in the kitchen and the door unlocked for you.

Sapphire waited for her to turn the light on and move out of the kitchen before she made her way to the decking. She'd never do anything to get her sisters into trouble. She was just pulling her shirt over her head when Sapphire spoke to her again.

I don't think he'll be back, do you? She didn't wait for an answer but continued. *I really made him mad, but he pissed me off too. He....*

She wasn't going to say anything else, but Diamond asked, *He what, Sapphire? What did he do to you to make you so hurt?*

He didn't want me. I mean at all. Instead of having sex with me, he...he did it himself, then told me to get dressed like I was some prostitute he'd just had and was finished with. She felt her anger rising again. *He said me being naked around him was hard on him. Like I was undressed because I'd taken my towel off. And I didn't invite him to my room. He came up there.*

Diamond was quiet as Sapphire made it up the stairs without being seen. It wasn't until she locked the door behind her and looked at the clock that she realized how late it was. Midnight. She'd been outside for nearly three hours.

So the two of you aren't mated? The question startled her. She knew that they'd not had sex, no intercourse at least. But what he'd done to her, did that mean he was marked? Probably not. Men of her kind did the marking, not the females.

No, we're not. She lay down on the bed as she continued to talk to her sister. *I have to go back to the other house tomorrow. I have to sign off on it for the new owners. I should be there and back in no time. But…. But I might stay for a couple of days. I was going to see if the job offer from Bruce is still open. He said I could work from here and only come into town once or twice a month.*

I guess you won't be able to work for Blair now either. That's too bad. I thought you could do wonders for his firm. She heard her sister sigh. *I'm going in for an interview in the morning. I have one at the hospital as an emergency room nurse. I think I'll enjoy it more than an office.*

They talked for a few more minutes, and Sapphire rolled to her back, just realizing that someone had made her bed. Picking up the pillow, she put it to her nose and could smell her grandmother. Smiling, she put it back and got up to look at the gifts her sisters had given her on the first day.

The one from Emerald was a framed picture of the two of them. She remembered the day it was taken and smiled. They'd been at the park running, just the two of them. The next gift was from Opal. It was a journal. She touched the pretty cover and knew that her sister had made it, stitching it from things she'd made something larger from. Opal made a good living from crafting things out of scraps of this and that. Diamond had given her a Kindle Fire. And with it was a gift card from Jade for her to download books. She picked up the gift from Ruby.

She'd framed one of her art pieces. It was of her; Sapphire knew this and could see her sister while Sapphire had sat for the painting. Sapphire had been tired and wanted to be left alone to take a nap, and Ruby had told her to simply go to sleep and she'd wake her when she was done. But she'd not been able to keep from watching her sister work. She was lovely when she was in her zone.

Crawling back into the bed, she avoided the bathroom because she knew it would smell like him. Some of his scent was perfuming the bedroom now. But after an hour in the bed, she realized she'd either have to use it or go down the hall and maybe encounter one of her sisters. She wasn't up for dealing with them tonight.

His scent hit her like a strong storm. Even the hand towel smelled like him, and she tossed it into the hamper after taking it to her nose several times. She was so pissed at him again that she was afraid she'd never sleep when she finally got back into her bed. Closing her eyes, she felt her body tighten and need for him to touch her curl around her body. Frustrated both sexually and mentally, she got up and showered. She might as well get started.

The sun was coming up when she pulled out of the drive. She was glad that the rest of them hadn't been downstairs when she left. It would have been hard on them, not to mention one of them would have called Blair, and she'd just as soon not have to deal with his ass today. Or the rest of her life. She was on the highway when her phone started ringing. When it finished ringing, she pulled over for a cup of tea, and, ignoring the voicemail, she turned it off and put it deep into her purse. She was going to enjoy this if it killed her.

Chapter 6

"Don't, Dad. I'm begging you not to say a word." Blair had been in his office for ten minutes when his dad walked in. And after the past three days, he wasn't sure he wouldn't snap again.

"I was just wondering if you know where she is yet. I've tried getting something out of Annabelle, but she's very closed mouthed. She does make a delicious apple pie, but will keep her mouth shut when it comes to those girls of hers." He sat down, and Blair groaned. He wanted everyone to leave him alone, but no one seemed to be listening to him.

Not even Diamond would tell him anything. And no matter how much he threatened the rest of them, no one would tell him where she was. It was as if she'd vanished into thin air. His phone ringing startled him.

"So you couldn't make her an offer she couldn't refuse, could you?" It took Blair a few seconds to realize who was talking. "She's a mighty hard woman to get to agree to anything when she has her mind set on it, isn't she?"

"Who?" He knew as soon as Bruce laughed. "Sapphire? You've talked to her? When? Where?"

"She came to see me a couple of days ago, and we just now got things worked out. She's coming in today to sign a contract with me. I tell you, I'm thrilled because I didn't realize how shitty my other employees were until then." Blair took a sheet of paper from his pad, scribbled on it, and handed it to his dad as Bruce continued. "She's taking a cut in pay, too, because she won't be here daily, but then I have to pay her mileage when I have to have her here."

"You do know she has a contract with me, right? She did mention that, didn't she?" Bruce laughed, and Blair knew that she had. "I'm not going to break it with her for this."

"She said you and her had a parting of ways. Said you'd more than likely be glad to see the back of her." He laughed again. "Seemed kind of like a personal thing, but she said it wasn't. Was it, Henson? Have you feelings for the young woman?"

His dad came back in and nodded at him. "I'll be there in an hour. What time is your meeting with her?"

"Two hours, but I can delay it if you really need me to, but it'll cost you." He sat up, almost afraid to hear what he wanted. "I would like to have her land an account for me. The client wants her, and only her. You let her work this one for me and I'll hold her here until you get here."

"Done. And if she's there when I get there I'll help see about shuffling a couple of accounts I have coming in your way. If she's willing to speak to me."

Bruce laughed. "You must have really pissed her off. Damn, but this is going to be fun to watch. All right, Henson, I'll sweet talk her for you. But you fuck this up with her and I'll not only have her in my company, but I'll tie her up for the next fifty years."

Blair said nothing and hung up. The man wouldn't live fifty minutes after he got there if he touched her. He looked at his dad as he pulled his jacket off the hanger and his dad started reading from a sheet of paper.

"The chopper is ready when you get there. I'm having Justine set you up in a hotel, bridal suite mind you, for when you woo her back here. And you'd better, too, or so help me I'll—"

"Nothing has changed, Dad. I still don't want a mate." He looked at his dad and hated the look of hurt on his face. "Even if I did, then it wouldn't be someone like Sapphire. In this type of business there can't be any waves made, and she'll make them for me."

"Then why are you bothering to go and get her? Just let her alone before she hurts you again or you hurt her. Blair, this isn't right. You have to know that." He picked up his briefcase and stopped when his dad stepped in front of him. "Don't do this, son. I'm begging you. Just leave her alone before it's too late."

"I can't. I have to make sure she realizes who the boss is." He slipped into the limo that had been parked out front and was on the move when he thought of what his dad had asked him to do. He had to make her understand that he was in charge of her.

The chopper was running when he moved across the tarmac. He was buckling in when he felt his dad reach for him. He wasn't sure what else could be said about this, but he knew his dad was worried about him.

She's a good girl. And I want you to know that if you do this to her, bring her back here without her consent, or worst yet, without her permission, you'll never win her love. He wanted to tell his dad he didn't want her love but for her to listen to him. But that wasn't right either.

Dad, you don't understand. That man who's after her won't stop until she's dead or he takes her back. What do you think will happen then? What do you suppose he'll do to her if he gets her back to his pack? He waited for an answer, and when his dad answered him, Blair felt his heart ache.

You do this and I'll never speak to you again. I'm not kidding, Blair. I love you very much. But you hurt this young girl because of some macho bullshit that you have to be in charge, and then I'll never talk to you again. The connection between then severed, and he felt a pain like he'd never felt before. He tried reaching for him again and again before he landed and he wouldn't answer. He was reaching for his phone when it rang. He nearly dropped it twice trying to answer it before it went to voicemail.

Justine told him when he called her that his dad wasn't coming to the phone. "Not that I blame him. If I didn't need this job, I'd not answer either. What are you thinking? That woman has done nothing to you."

She hadn't, either. He'd done everything to her. He waited for her to stop yelling at him as he thought about what he was doing. Really? What was he doing here? Did he really expect no less from her than her to run? He had forced her hand, and now she was leaving him. He thought of the look on her face when he'd told her to get dressed. He knew that he'd hurt her and had felt the pain of it every time he thought of it.

"I don't know what's wrong with me." Justine snorted, and he realized he'd spoken out loud. "I don't want a mate. She's beautiful and smart, but I just don't have time to train one right now."

That hadn't come out right, but before he could revise his comment, Justine started in on him. He just let her, knowing that every word she said to him was no less than he deserved.

"Train her? I see, and do you want me to go to your apartment when you return with her and put out a doggie basket and piddle papers for her? Do you think it'll be hard to paper train her, or do you plan to let her out in the yard when she has to pee? Oh wait, that won't work, you only have an apartment. At least 'untrainable' Sapphire has a home that she paid for, a truck that she owns, and sisters she's put through college." He opened his mouth to speak when she cut him off. "You've lived in the apartment with the same maid service since I've known you, and I bet you my next check that you have no idea what her name is."

He didn't, he realized. "What the hell does this have to do with Sapphire and her not listening to me?"

"You don't, do you? What about her sisters? Do you know their names? Do you know her grandmother's name?" He told her their names as well as her grandmother. "So in one month you've not only found a mate that you don't want, you've gained the family that comes with her. And for the life of you you've no idea what the woman's name is that has cleaned your apartment for the past fifteen years."

He closed his phone when she hung up on him. He leaned back in the limo and tried to think what the fuck he really was doing. He realized that as much as he needed to prove a point when he left his office, for the life of him he couldn't remember what the hell it had been.

Did he want her? Yes, he did. In his bed, on the floor, in the shower, anywhere he could have her. Did he need her? That one was a little harder to answer. No, not really.

Then why did he pursue her? Why did he need so desperately to bring her in line? Why did he feel the need to protect her at all costs? He knew that she was brave. Hell, he thought after what her sister had told him she was a great deal braver than him. She'd taken more chances in the little time that he'd known her than he had in the last ten years.

He looked up at his driver, a man he knew was a tiger. "Lucas, are you mated? Do you have a mate at home now?"

The man looked at him in the mirror, then back at the road before answering him. "My missus passed some years back. We had a long, but not nearly long enough life before she left me behind. Why do you ask, sir?"

"The woman I'm going after now, she's my mate. I don't want her, I don't need her, either, but I can't seem to help myself in trying to drag her back to me. And she doesn't seem to want me, either." Lucas snorted and glanced at him again. "You think I'm an ass, too, right? A prick because I don't want what is supposed to be the other half of me."

"No, sir, I don't. You got your reasons, I'm sure. I didn't want a mate, either, when I met my Clare. She was just the opposite of me. Outspoken, had an opinion a mile and a half long, and a body that would stop a train on a runaway track. So, nope, didn't want her at all. The harder I pushed her away, the harder she ran from me. Didn't do her no good, 'course. I kept sniffing around her until one day I realized it."

Blair waited, knowing that he was going to say something like he realized he loved her or that he found that life without her was something he didn't care to contemplate. But when Lucas stopped at the next light and turned to look at him, he knew it was going to be something from his heart and the man had shared this with no one else before.

"I realized then that she didn't need me any more than I needed her. That when it was all said and done, like them fates are saying to us, she was the only one in the world that was going to ever love me like I wanted to be loved." The horn blared from behind him, but still he sat looking at him. "Mr. Henson, that woman you want, she got something besides her body you want? A baby you planted there? Money she might bring to the table?"

"No. Stubbornness, same mouthyness that your missus had, I'm sure, and a body that would make a man whimper for only a small glimpse of it. She's smart, strong, and took on an alpha twice her size to save her family." Lucas nodded and turned back around. When he glanced at him again after moving in the traffic, he winked at him.

"Then I'd advise you to go on up there, get down on your knees, and beg her to forgive you. Don't matter that you don't think you did wrong. You more'n likely did to her way of thinking. You got yourself a woman who'd die for you and more'n likely kill for you, too. If, and this here is a big if, you can let her be the same woman she is now, and twenty, maybe even fifty years from now, you'll have a woman that can't help but want you. 'Cause I gotta tell you, security might be good for your office and such, but a woman who would kill for you while you're between her legs, that's the woman I'd want by my side for the rest of my days."

Blair sat back in his seat and thought about it. Never once did he say he had to love her because he was supposed to. Lucas had told him that she'd protect him, not the other way around. Did he need protecting by her? More than likely not. A woman like her would need to be protected if from no one else but from herself.

"I need to stop and pick up some flowers." Lucas shook his head. "You think flowers would be wrong or we can't stop?"

"She kicked that alpha's ass, you said, then she don't need flowers. No, a girl like her would need something else. Something to show that you trust her. What is it a wolf like you is more afraid of than having your next deal go sour?"

Lucas stopped the car in front of a pawn shop and got out and opened his door. There were all kinds of signs in the window. Most of them bright with neon and a few of them hand written. Blair looked at the one sign that seemed to scream at him "danger."

Without a word to the man, he walked into the shop, hoping to Christ he didn't just sign his own death certificate. The man at the counter seemed to recognize him as an alpha and asked him what he could do for him. Blair took a deep breath and told him just what he wanted.

~~~

Sapphire looked at her watch again. She'd been told ten minutes about an hour ago. Either Bruce wanted her or not. She wanted to go home tonight and sleep in her own bed. She glanced up when the elevator opened. She was standing up when the one man in the world she didn't want to see walked toward her.

"What the fuck are you...he called you." Blair didn't move, and he didn't scream and demand like she thought he would. He nodded and asked her to have a seat please. She didn't move.

"I would like to speak to you, please, before you make the decision to work for Bruce. And, yes, he called me for no other reason than to cover his own ass. He knew we had a contract, and he didn't want to lose his shirt over it." She sat, but wasn't sitting back all comfortable like he appeared to be.

He looked at the secretary, and she moved out of the area. She wondered for a moment what it would be like to have such power that with only a look you could make people do your bidding. Blair turned back to her and put a bag in her hand.

"What is this?" She held the weight of it in her hand and wondered what sort thing he'd bring her. Probably a bottle of poison, and he was going to demand that she drink it down. When he cleared his throat, she looked up at him.

"Please open it. I bought it for you because I want to show you...I want you to trust me. I want to trust you, as well." She reached for the box that was deep in the bag and opened it. If he noticed that her hands were shaking, he didn't comment. When she looked at the contents, she looked at him.

"I don't understand." He nodded and took out the switchblade and opened it. The silver blade seemed to spark in the room. "You bought me a silver knife. Why? So I'd kill myself with it and be out of your misery?"

She flushed when he looked hurt. "No, I bought it because, like I said, I want to show you that I trust you. Not just the knife, but with decisions, too. I should have...I've treated you badly, and I want to make up for it."

"Why?" She could tell he was struggling with his temper, and for some reason that made her feel good. She wanted him to struggle with it and not lash out at her like she was stupid.

"I'm sorry. When you came into the bathroom that morning—" She started to cut him off, but he raised his hand. "Please, you asked me, and I'm trying to explain. I was embarrassed that you caught me doing something very childish. Something that men don't like to be caught doing."

"I thought it was sexy." She watched his wolf stir along his skin and felt her own wolf as well. "That doesn't mean I want you or want to have sex with you. I just thought it was kind of sexy. Nothing more."

"Do you have any idea how much I wanted you to touch me? How much, right now, I'd like to press you back against that chair and taste you again?" Her body tightened, and she squeezed her thighs together so he couldn't smell her. "Don't close me off. Let me have your scent right now."

She was playing with fire, and they both knew it. Opening her legs just a little, she saw his nostrils flare, and she moaned softly. When he ran his hand up between her legs, she let him, knowing that the game they were playing—and it was just a game—was going to hurt them both.

His fingers brushed against her pussy, and she opened wider for him. He moved then, blocking her from the elevator and the desk in front of her. When he slipped his fingers under the elastic of her panties, she put her hand on his forearm and he stopped immediately.

"This is wrong." He nodded and stayed where he was. "You don't want me. You were sickened by my body and my wounds. You turned me away."

"I was a fool, and I wasn't sickened by anything about you. Your taste was more than I'd ever dreamed of before. Your body, all I could think about was how perfect you were, beautiful and all mine." She shook her head. "You don't believe me?"

"I don't know what to believe from you. For all I know, you could just want to masturbate again to relieve some tension in you so you can forget me ten minutes later." He shook his head this time. "Blair, we're not going to be good for each other. You have to know that."

"All I know right now is that I want you in my bed, every morning and every night. You've no idea what your words do to me. No clue how much I'd like to find a table, lay you out over it and come all over you. Then drink from you again until I'm full. Then I'd like to pull you over my cock and slowly enter you, move inside of you, stretching you until I'm buried to my balls. I want to fuck you slowly, taste your nipples in my mouth and—" She moaned as he slid his fingers under her panties and into her sheath. "Come for me. Come right now and let me lick my fingers clean of you before I have to take you right here."

She held onto his arm as she came, holding her other hand over her mouth while she screamed out against it. When he moved her hand and took her mouth, she felt his fingers move over her clit, and she forgot she didn't like him, didn't think about the fact that she knew that this was wrong and was going to hurt them. All she wanted, all she needed was right here, right now.

Again, he whispered through her mind, and she felt her body respond to him as though he owned her. She didn't want to be owned by anyone. But it was a moot point, she supposed, when the die had been cast.

When he slid his hand from her, she looked at him. Her heart was pounding, and her body wanted more. When he leaned into her neck and nipped at her ear, she had to hold onto him because she was sure she was going to fall, and she was sitting down.

"Would you like a minute?" She nodded. "I can go in and talk to Bruce until you come in. I'll be waiting for you." He stood up, and she looked at him, and then watched as he cupped his cock and moaned. "I ache, but having you like this makes it worth it. To watch you come is almost more than a man can stand." Leaning down, he kissed her mouth quickly and stood up. When he put his fingers in his mouth and sucked them, she looked at his cock. She wanted to taste him in the worst kind of way.

"Go to the bathroom before I forget again where we are and take you right here." She nodded and he helped her stand up. She looked into his eyes and saw the need she was feeling looking back at her. When he turned her and gave her a little push, she felt strangely sexy and wanton. Sapphire wondered if they ever got to a bed if it would feel this fucking good. His low growl made her slow her step and put more twist in her ass. He growled again, and she smiled. This was amazing.

Chapter 7

Blair stood up when she came in the room. He wanted to take her to the floor and have his way with her, but only took her hand and led her to her seat. Bruce had explained to him what he wanted from Sapphire, and he was hard pressed to not tell the man she'd be working for him, not Bruce. When she sat down, he did as well and took a slow easy breath.

"Bruce has a client he wants to work with you on. If you'd be willing to do that for him, I'd like to talk to you about a partnership. With the two of us." He glanced at Bruce, who looked like he was excited. "I need your expertise, and so does Bruce. I think the best way to handle this is that we share you. In business dealings. If you would like."

He was working off the top of his head. He could see a shit load of benefits from this...and a lot of pitfalls, too. Where could she stay when working here in town where he'd feel like she was safe? Which one of them would take precedence over the other if a project needed something and she was working with the other? He tried to seem as calm as he usually did in business deals, but this one had the most at stake.

"What happens if a client wants something else when I'm working for the other partner?" He nearly smiled at her, loving the fact that she wasn't going to just say no. "And who decides which ones I work on with whom?"

He looked at Bruce, hoping the man was going to be okay with this. He wasn't sure about this and nearly bluffed his way through it to get what he wanted, but he was trying to change. For her, he realized.

"I don't know." He'd never uttered those words in a deal meeting in his life. "We'll have to work out the bumps as we go. We'd have to figure out your pay, vacation, and retirement...all the perks that one of us would give you if you worked for us singly. Then there are going to be things we've never thought of, things that I'm sure will try the relationship, but I think this could work to both our benefits."

"I like it, too. I'll be able to take on a few of the bigger clients that I couldn't with the staff I have now, and with Sapphire working for both of us we'll both save money too." Bruce smiled at them both and leaned back in his chair. "So, can we get together tomorrow night for dinner and see what our lawyers can come up with as a working plan?"

Too fast, too fast, his mind screamed at him. He wanted to plan, to write out lists. Blair wanted to do cost studies and work around making it so that all the t's were crossed and i's dotted. He looked at Sapphire, and she was looking at him, and a calmness came over him like he'd never had before.

"I think we can make that. That is if Sapphire is in agreement." He wasn't sure, but he thought he heard Bruce laugh. "You want to stay here one more night before you go back home?"

"I could do that. If my room isn't taken already. I'd already checked out, you see." She looked nervous then, and he could hear her heart pounding. "I might have to bunk with you if you have the room."

He nodded, unable to think how to respond without dropping to his knees and begging her to bunk with him. In his bed. Blair cleared this throat and shifted. He was hurting again. When she looked at him, he licked his lips and could taste her there. He felt his wolf snarl at him to take her now.

"How about dinner?" Blair looked at Bruce when he spoke. He had no idea what the man was talking about, and he thought he knew it. "Dinner? I'm sure the two of you have worked up an appetite. I know I have."

Blair had an appetite all right, and his dinner was sitting next to him. When she moved on the chair, he could smell her then. She was aroused, and he opened his mouth to take in more of her.

"I'd like some dinner." Blair stood when she did and walked behind her to the door. He didn't have a clue where they were going, but he followed her anyway. "How about if we go to that fast-food place on Linden Avenue? I don't think it's far from here."

"Oh no, this is cause for a celebration. My treat. We'll go to Muddy Misers. They have steak and the best ribs in the state." Bruce moved them both to the elevator and pressed the button for down as he continued. "They have these sweet potato fries that are drizzled with brown sugar and butter. Fabulous, just fabulous."

Dinner was a blur. It was good, he supposed, because before he realized it he had a cleaned plate in front of him. And there were only a few crumbs on his bread plate. He'd been drinking water since they sat down because Sapphire had, and there were several empty glasses on the table. But right now he wanted to leave. When Sapphire stood to use the ladies' room, Blair looked at Bruce when he laughed.

"You've got it bad, don't you?" Blair didn't even pretend to not know what he was talking about and nodded. "How long have you two been together?"

"We've...I'm not...." He looked around the restaurant. "I don't know how we got here or what I had to eat. I haven't a clue what our waitress looks like or even if we had one. Sapphire is all I can think about, and I'm afraid of fucking this up. Does that answer your question?"

"Yeah, it does. And this uncertainty looks good on you." Blair frowned at him, not understanding. "You are the most self-assured, confident man I've ever had the pleasure to work with. Right now, I'm seeing you for the man I know you really are and not the hard-assed prick everyone else sees in you." Bruce stood up and took the check. "You want to keep that woman, you show her this side of you more often. You might be able to keep her if you do."

With that, he walked away. When Sapphire was walking toward him, he stood up and watched her. She didn't seem to be any surer of herself than he was right now. When she got close to him, he helped her into her jacket and handed her the purse that was hanging on the back of her chair. Without a word, he walked her out of the restaurant and into the waiting limo. As soon as the door closed, he pulled her to him and rolled her to the seat.

~~~

Sapphire felt as if she were drowning in emotions. Every time he touched her, ran his hand against her, she felt her skin vibrate and hum with pleasure. When he sat up and pulled her over his lap, she straddled him. She could feel his hard length beneath her and moved over him slowly.

"I'm going to come if you keep that up. And I'd very much like to be naked with you when that happens." His voice did things to her that had her wanting him to come, anyway she could have him. "Sapphire, honey, I don't want to hurt you, but if you keep this up we're never leaving this limo tonight. And as much as I'd like to be deep inside of you right now, making love to you in the back seat of a car is not the way I'd like to do it our first time."

"I ache for you." He moaned and bit her breast through her blouse and bra. "Please, Blair. I don't know what's happening here, but I need more. Give it to me."

He ran his hand up under her skirt and slammed his fingers into her. Gone was the gentle touch; they were well beyond that, and she knew it. Riding him hard now, she pulled her blouse free of her skirt and up over her bra. He growled at her as he lifted the lace up and took as much of her as he could into his mouth. When he sucked hard on her, she cried out and curled her fingers into his hair. She wasn't sure if it was to hold him there or to hang on.

"I need you." He growled at her again, his words fueling her on. "We're not going to make it. Christ, I need you now."

He moved her back on his lap and opened his pants. His cock nearly leapt from him. She couldn't believe how thick he was, how hard he looked. When he told her to sit up on her knees, she did so, and he lifted her skirt over her hips, put his hands around her hips, and held her panties.

"If you want to stop, now is the time to say so. Once I tear these from you, I'm going to be inside of you, and it'll be too late." She nodded. "No, say it. I want to hear you say that you want me to take you. Say it or I stop now."

She was breathing so hard it hurt. She wanted him. She needed him. Not wanting to think about what this would mean for them, she nodded and took his mouth hard before lifting her head and looking him in the eye.

"Do it. Take me now." He tore her panties away, the last barrier between him and her. When he lifted her up, he kissed her and held her above him. She felt her pussy heat more, and when he bought her down slowly, the thick head of his cock right at her entrance, she started to tell him she was afraid. But he pulled her down so hard and so fast that she screamed before she had a chance to say anything.

Sapphire buried her face in his shoulder. She hurt, and hurt badly. She wanted him to let her go, to tell him to…pull away, but she was afraid it would hurt more. When she realized he was speaking, she lifted her head to understand.

"I didn't know." She tried to look away from him because he sounded so pissed off again. "I'm really sorry, baby. I just didn't…I didn't think that you'd be a virgin."

She looked at him sharply and snapped back. "Did you think I slept with anyone that came along? I'll have you know that I didn't even date all that much because of the way men made me feel—" He cut her off by putting his hand over her mouth.

"I didn't mean that either. I meant that I'd've never dreamed a man, any man, wouldn't have convinced you to have sex with him. Christ, you're beautiful when you're pissed." She started to move, trying to get away from him looking at her so intently when she felt his hands grip her hips. "Don't move, please. I'm barely hanging on here, and you've got me so deep inside of you it's difficult not to want to come."

"You like this?" He nodded and chuckled. "It's not all that much...your fingers were much better than—" He moved her with his hands, a rocking motion that rubbed her clit in a way that she saw stars. "Again."

His hands moved her as he suckled at her nipples. First one, then the other, until she was dizzy with need. When he cupped her ass and brought her even harder over him, she moaned.

"I want to roll you to your back on the seat. When I do, wrap your legs around me like you did the other day." She nodded, hoping that this never ended, and when it did that it felt like it did when he touched her.

When she was on her back, she couldn't believe the pleasure she got from this, from him. Wrapping her legs around him only brought him closer, deeper inside of her, until she was sure she could feel him at the back of her throat.

"Come for me, Sapphire. Please, baby, let go and take me with you." She tilted her head and gave him her throat. When his tongue licked across her shoulder, she came. Not hard, but a quick punch to her system that had her needing more. Rolling her hips upward, she felt his shudder and did it again. He put his hand over her mouth and sank his teeth into her shoulder.

Screaming, she bit down hard on his hand as she cried out her release. Her body seemed to explode over and over until she saw her vision blur. When he roared against her throat, she came again, her entire being seemed to come apart and shatter, only to come back together in a vibrating sensation of completion.

He wasn't heavy on her, but felt...she supposed *right* would have been the word to use about his weight over her.

When he lifted his head and looked down at her, she felt suddenly embarrassed.

"I'm sorry," he said. She looked up at him as he pulled away from her. "This was neither the time nor the place to do this in. But you looked so delicious that I couldn't help myself."

He'd hurt her again. She wasn't sure what he'd said that made her heart feel as if he'd stabbed her, but she sat up and moved to the other side of the seat. She'd forgotten, if she thought about it, that they were in a moving car. She adjusted her clothes and tried to act like this sort of thing happened to her all the time.

"Where is your hotel? I'm going to have to go to the one on Sales Avenue. My things are there." She looked up at him when he didn't answer her. "What?"

"You're staying with me, right? I've made arrangements for you and me to stay together." She nearly said okay, but he continued. "It would be stupid of you to pay for another room when I have a perfectly good one at the Royal."

"Maybe I prefer being stupid over being with you in the same room." She felt her temper rise and tried to pull it back. "This was a major mistake. I let my hormones dictate what happened here, and now I realize how idiotic it was. I'd very much like for you to take me to my hotel, and I'll meet you tomorrow at—"

"No." She didn't say anything but looked out the window, trying very hard not to knock the shit out of him. "Look, we're both embarrassed. We'll go to the hotel, my hotel, and sleep on it. Then in the morning we'll make the arrangements for you to move into my apartment and then have the—"

"I'm not moving in with you." He started to speak, but she cut him off again. "I have a house, a family to care for. I'm not living in some apartment building where I can't run when I want to and not see my sisters when I want. We can...we can simply meet at work, and if you want to do this again, then we'll find a hotel. But I'm not living with you."

"You most certainly will." His voice thundered in the car, and she was a little afraid. But he was not going to order her around. "You'll do as I say on this. I'm willing to be a little less strict on you about your job and things, but I will not have you living away from me where I can't keep an eye on you."

"Keep an eye on me? What for? Do you think I'm going to go out now and find another male to fuck me?" He flushed. "You son of a bitch, you think that, don't you?"

Sapphire rolled the window down between her and the driver. She was sure he heard everything that had happened behind him, but he only nodded at her when the divider was down. Blair didn't say a word to her, but glared.

"Could you please take me to the Grace Hotel on Sales?" When Blair finally started to speak, she looked at him. "If you say one word to me, one, I will shift and tear you apart. If you think I'm kidding, then try it."

She heard the driver swallow but never took her eyes off Blair. She knew he was a tiger and would understand that he'd be hurt, maybe killed, if she did what she promised. When Blair nodded, she sat back against the opposite door from him and looked out the darkened window. She wasn't going to stay there. She was going home. And if he thought to make other arrangements for her again, she'd fucking kill him.

The rest of her trip was made in silence. When the limo stopped, she was out before the driver was and hurried into the hotel to where she knew they'd been holding her bags. She stood at the desk and waited until the car pulled away before she pulled out her cell phone.

"Diamond, I'm coming home. Could you please...?" She had to take several deep breaths before she could continue. "Could you please do me a favor and call a lawyer? I need someone who is savvy in real-estate law."

"What happened? You know I'll do anything for you, but you have to tell me what happened." She couldn't answer her sister, and she seemed to understand. "Will you tell me before you make any rash decisions?" Her sister touched her mind, and Sapphire closed the phone and asked for her things when Diamond told her she loved her.

I have to leave. The house is paid for, and you'll be fine. She sobbed slightly making the staff move away from her. *I'm his mate, but he doesn't trust me. He wants me to live with him in the apartment because...because he thinks I'll find another male to fuck me.*

The management had been very nice to her, and she felt the need to thank them but couldn't stop crying. The manager came out to help her load her things into her car and asked her several times if he could help her.

"I'm fine, thank you," she told him. "Just lost something very important and now I'm going home."

He was still standing there when she pulled into traffic. Diamond called her back a few minutes later, and she didn't answer. She should have known that wouldn't work. She and Diamond were as close as sisters could be.

I've called for you and made an appointment with this guy I met at the hospital this morning. I got the job, by the way. I start Monday. Now tell me everything.

Sapphire

It took her nearly a box of tissues and two hours of her four-hour trip to tell her everything. Sapphire had wanted to leave out the part about the sex but wanted her to know that he'd not raped her when she'd asked.

He was very gentle with me. I'm sure it could have been a lot worse. She flushed when she thought about riding him and changed the subject. *He can find me now, can't he?*

Yes. You can him as well now that you've exchanged...fluids. I would guess that as arrogant as he is, he more than likely thinks you're back at the hotel sobbing your eyes out. He'll be just stupid enough to think you'll wait for him. She snorted at her. *Sapphire, I swear to you when I went to talk to him the other day, I never thought this would happen.*

Diamond had told her about the conversation she'd had with Blair and that she'd thought he'd try. Well, he did, all right. Just long enough for him to get what he wanted. And now...now she had no idea what to do because she had a feeling that even though she'd threatened him, she really couldn't hurt him. Not physically anyway. A plan started to form in her mind, and she smiled.

I know you didn't, but what's done is done. But do you remember that guy we met when we first came up here to see the house? The gay guy, the one who let us sleep in his bed when the bed and breakfast was closed for the week? She said she did. *You think he'd play at being my date a few times?*

I think you'll get him killed if you do that. That's not very nice anyway. Why would you stoop to his level? Blair just isn't worth it. Sapphire agreed with her. She wasn't going to get anyone hurt because she'd been broken.

And she had been, too. Not just by Blair, but by Jeffery and even Bruce. He'd called Blair and set her up. Jeffery had simply betrayed her as her alpha, and Blair…Blair had crushed her. She was pulling into the long drive of their home when she came to a decision. Diamond was sitting on the porch with Grandmother when she got out of the car.

"I'm going to go into business for myself. I'm going to call it Marketing Gems. And I'm going to knock Blair on his ass with my business sense." Her grandmother hugged her and told her "good girl."

"You think this is a good idea?" Diamond asked her as she helped her bring her things up. "It's like waving a red flag in front of a raging bull."

"I hope so. I certainly hope so." She took a long shower after her sister left for her room. No one but her and Grandmother knew she was home, and she hoped to keep it that way for a little while longer. She had things to do.

By midnight she was crawling into bed, exhausted but happy with what she'd been able to begin. Her name was now hers as she'd applied for a patent on it, business cards were designed, and she'd take them to the printer tomorrow. And she had her first client. At least she hoped that Opal would let her market her things for her.

Closing her eyes, Sapphire was quite proud of herself. She'd only thought of Blair about fifty times in the six hours she'd been working and had been able to ignore the fact that since he'd mated with her, all her wounds were now healed. Finally a perk, she thought.

Chapter 8

Jeffery wasn't going to forget this. He looked at the pictures that he'd had an investigator take of Sapphire. The one of her and Henson getting into the limo had him wanting to find them both and make them suffer. Even a fool could see that they'd had sex, and they couldn't keep their hands off each other even then.

"When was this taken?" He looked up when his enforcer, Harris, didn't answer. "I asked you a question, and I expect an answer. When the fuck were these taken?"

"Yesterday. Late evening. They were driven around for a good hour before they were lost in the crowd at the gallery that had opened. He lost which limo was theirs. He found it in front of the Royal Hotel half an hour later, but they had both gone in by then." Harris sat up in the chair, seemingly almost relieved. "I'll call him off and bring the others in. I'm glad that this is over. You should have left them girls alone a long time ago, and we both know it."

"What's over? I never said this was finished. I want her more now than before. And that fucking prick Henson. They think they can just pretend that I didn't make a claim on her first and just get away with it? Hardly." He sat down behind his desk, still nursing his wounds. "The trial, what do you know about it?"

Harris was his brother, and to a point he could let him get by with some things, but huffing at him was not one of them. Before he could think how much pain it would cause him, he leapt at him and clawed at his face. He couldn't fight back because of him being his alpha, but that didn't stop Jeffery from nearly killing him.

"Get out." Harris shifted, and Jeffery had a moment of panic before his brother turned and left the office. When he was nearly out, he turned back to him and bared his teeth. The low growl made his skin crawl, and he had a feeling that, brother or not, he'd just made an enemy.

"Not the first and certainly not the last one I'll make," Jeffery said as he sat down. He had things to do, and he wanted them done yesterday if not before. If Harris didn't want to work with him, then he'd find someone who would. Traitors he didn't need. He needed men that wouldn't ask him how they were supposed to do something assigned them but come back with results. Besides, he'd be back. He always came back begging for another chance.

It took him almost an hour to find someone who could give him information on the trial with the Board of Weres, and that person was less than helpful. A stupid woman who kept telling him that there was no trial set up, and the date that he'd thought it was on was full of other issues. He'd finally had to snarl at her to shut the fuck up and listen to him.

"Give me your boss, you incompetent idiot. Women like you give wolves a bad name." She huffed, and he wanted to hang up and go down there and beat the living shit out of her, but knew in his current condition she'd hurt him more than he could her. When her boss, or what she'd said was her boss, came on, Jeffery was in a vile mood.

"Are there any men working in that office?" She, a Miss Hoover, didn't answer. "You do know what a man is, don't you? Your superior in all ways. The one that signs your paycheck?"

He sat there for two minutes waiting for someone else when his phone suddenly told him that if he wanted to make a call to please hang up and dial again. He realized then that the fucking cunt had hung up on him. He slammed the phone in the cradle only to snatch it up again and snarl at the caller when it rang almost immediately. He was going to rip the head off this person if it was the last thing he did.

"You called here and needed information on a trial," the person started on the other end without much in the way of introductions. "Well, you want it, then you do what everyone else does, come down here and fill out the paperwork. We'll try our best to get it back to you within twenty-four to forty-eight hours." The man at the other end was short and pissed. Jeffery took a deep breath before he answered the man.

"I was only upset because she didn't have the information I needed. This trial was about one of my pack members attacking me, and she didn't have a clue what I wanted or anything on that date. I just want this finished because Sapphire is an alpha in her own right, though I have no idea how true this is because she is only a female, but the injuries she gave me are not healing. I'm sorry for my short fuse, but I do hurt a great deal." He could hear papers shuffling on his end and smiled. "Please tell Miss Hoover that I'm not usually so mean to the working woman."

No, he was usually meaner if he noticed them at all. When he heard the man mumble something about answering the phone and dealing with idiots, Jeffery had to bite his tongue. Didn't these people know who he was? Apparently not.

"The trial has been cancelled. Due to her finding another alpha and being claimed by him. The paperwork filed an hour ago claims that Sapphire Erickson and Blair Henson, Alpha have mated and bonded so she is now your equal and no longer the subject of any investigation." The man laughed. "I guess you're just shit out of luck today."

"That's not right. She wasn't my equal when she hurt me." He tried to think of dates of anything that would help him. "She can't have been claimed by Henson anyway. I want her for my own bitch."

"You'll have to take that up with her mate then. But you yourself said she was an alpha and would have been long before she mated to Blair. You, as her first alpha, should have recognized that and made arrangements to have her removed before you and she tangled." The man laughed again. "You must be more stupid than anyone here thinks you are."

The line went dead, and he was left with nothing. Damn it all to hell, this wasn't right and it wasn't going his way. Nothing was it seemed, and he was fucking sick of it. When the phone rang again, he was still trying to think what to do when he simply picked it up without checking to see who it was. It was the man from the Were offices again.

"It would seem that we have a trial for you, after all." Relieved, he sat back as the man continued. "The date is set for June the twenty-first at 7:45 in the morning. Can you be there?"

"I will. What do I need to bring for proof of what happened?" Jeffery picked up a pen and topped the sheet of paper with *"Cunts trial"* and put down the numbers one through ten. "I've pictures if you want them."

"That won't be necessary. We have all the pictures we need. We took these ourselves." Jeffery frowned. "And a statement. You might want to have one as well. It would expedite things if you did."

"All right, I can do that. But how did you get pictures? I've never…I don't believe there were any photos taken at the clinic where I was first treated. Unless, of course, you mean her pictures. I can assure you that all her wounds are nothing compared to the ones—"

"Her? There was a woman involved? Hang on." He seemed to be gone forever, and when he came back, he was laughing. "I'm sorry to inform you, Mr. Benetton, this has nothing to do with Mrs. Henson. This is a complaint filed by one Harris Benetton. I believe he's your brother as well as your one time enforcer. He said you tried to kill him this morning when he was in your office." The laughter is what snapped his temper. The man had no right to—Jeffery had to get this straightened out immediately. This was ridiculous.

"Let me talk to him," he snapped at the man. "I'll talk some sense into him, and this will be over. Of all the stupid…where is he? I want to speak to the moron. He can't file a complaint against his own alpha. Put him on the line." Laughter again, then the man had the nerve to have a sharp edge to his voice.

"I'm sorry, but I won't do that. I could really, we don't want to have this sort of thing putting the courts further behind, but after the abuse two of my employees had to suffer at your verbal attack this morning, I'm going to agree to this one. No reason for you to get by with too much, and frankly, I don't like you very much. You, sir, are a horrible man and should be put down."

For the third time already that day, he was hung up on.

~~~

Blair hung up his phone as gently as he could. He'd already broken one this morning, and if he threw this one across the room, Justine said she would quit. He didn't want her to do that, so he was trying his best to behave himself.

"No one at the house is answering the phone," Justine said. "I've called three times in the past hour. They don't even have voicemail set up or an answering machine." Justine eyed the phone as she continued. "Do you have any other number we can call?"

He didn't, not even a cell phone number. "I've got someone looking into seeing if she has a contract with anyone, but no luck so far. I tried the number that Bruce gave me as well, and she's not answering it, either."

"I know you think you didn't do anything wrong, but think. What did you say or do that has her running again? Because this is just what she's doing, running from you." He leaned back in his chair as he thought of what had happened yesterday and could now see he had fucked up. Again.

"I told her she was moving in with me, and she objected. Loudly." He looked at Justine when she laughed. "I can't control her. She won't let me."

"Well, of course you can't, and why would you want to? My god, Blair, she's a grown woman. Why do you think she needs controlling?" He didn't want to have to explain again how he couldn't protect her if she wasn't near him when Justine latched onto it anyway. "You think she's not going to be able to protect herself against Jeffery? Or you for that matter? The woman is an alpha. You said so

90

yourself. What the hell were you thinking of doing, keeping her on a leash for the rest of her life so you could jerk her back if she strayed too far away from big, bad Blair Henson?"

"You make me sound like a Neanderthal. I'm more evolved than that." She snorted. "I have run a very successful business for a number of years. I'm not stupid, you know."

"Then act like it." She stood up. "Has your father spoken to you yet? I've been trying to reach him, too, since he stormed out of here yesterday. I think he's pissed at you too."

He was. His dad had been thrilled to death when he'd come into the office yesterday. He could smell her on him, he'd told Blair. When he asked where she was so he could hug her too, Blair had been too pissed off to try and smooth over what had happened so his dad wouldn't be mad too.

"She's left me. Just packed up her shit and left me hanging. We were going to go into business together. Bruce and our lawyer had worked all night on a contract that would benefit him and me, and when she was called to come and look it over before she signed it, we were told she was gone." He waited for his dad to agree with him, but he shook his head before saying anything.

"This contract, it was written by you and Bruce's lawyers, so how much input did she have in it?" He didn't get the chance to answer before his dad went on. "And as much as I hate to ask you this, because as surely as I'm sitting here, I'm hoping the answer is better than I think. Where did you mate with that poor girl at?"

"She was just as needy as I was." He'd felt stupid at his outburst and still did. "We were in the back of the limo

91

when it happened. I had planned to make it up to her when she went back to the hotel with me."

"Your hotel, no doubt." He nodded, not liking how his dad was making him look. "And was there going to be flowers? Music? Maybe a bottle of champagne to make this up to her?"

His dad stood up and left his office without even waiting for an answer. Not that he had one to give him. Blair hadn't thought of those things. She'd been...she was his, and he'd taken her like a horny school kid and had pissed her off. And now his dad was, too.

"I have to fix this." Justine nodded and moved toward her desk. "Will you help me?"

"No. You're on your own now." She was putting on her jacket and picking up her purse when she looked at him. "You want this woman? Then I'd suggest you figure this out on your own. I'm finished trying to teach you how to be a good man. If you don't want her, and I mean the forever kind of want her, then I suggest you leave her alone. She can fend for herself, and I'm pretty sure she can kick your ass while she's at it."

He sat there for an hour, trying to think. He knew that he could be overbearing and bossy, but that was who he was. Why did everyone expect him to change and not her? He'd been...he'd been an ass, and he knew it, but she was pretty unbending, too. He stood up and decided to go to her house. She'd either let him in or not, but he had to try and fix this. If for no other reason than to make good with his dad.

The drive to her house didn't improve his mood much. He'd tried several times to call her but still got no answer. He was pulling in the driveway when it occurred to him that this was a done deal and he was going to be fucked if he didn't fix this. Actually, he should have known that sooner, he thought, but he was a slow learner when it came to women. Damn it all to hell, this was going to kill him, if she didn't first.

He knocked on the door twice. They were there, he was sure of it, but not letting him come in. He knew that they'd gang up on him, and he really didn't know why, but that sort of hurt. Blair was walking back to his car when he saw Annabelle in the garden in the back of the house. He walked around to see if she'd speak to him.

"She's pissed at you." He stopped walking and stood there while she continued hoeing. "I've never seen her so upset with anyone in my life, and I've known her since she was a cub. You might be better off just getting in the tiny little thing you call a car and getting out before someone realizes you're here and tries to kill you."

"I screwed up badly with her. But I don't know what to do when she pisses me off, too." He heard her laugh and dropped his head in shame. "I'm an asshole, but I don't mean to hurt her. I have no idea what I'm supposed to be doing with her or for her because whenever I get close enough to find out, I open my mouth and screw things up."

"Yes, you do, but admitting you're an idiot is the first step of many to the road to recovery. You messed up as badly as Jeffery, her old alpha did. But yours ran deeper." She stopped hoeing and turned to look at him. "She's starting her own business. And she'll make a go of it too, without your help. You should learn something from this in the event you get a second chance at having a mate again."

"She's not going to be my mate?" She shrugged and went back to work. "I would like your help. I know I have no right to ask this of you, but I'm going to try harder and not at pissing her off if I can help it. I guess she's going to give me a run for my money before I can even think to make it work with her, isn't she? I…my dad is a horrible flirt, and I worked so hard at not being him that I've forgotten how to be human around women."

That statement startled him. He'd never realized until just then how much he didn't want to be like his father when he was the greatest man he knew. Annabelle told him to get to work, and he bent to pick up a hoe. Taking off his jacket and tie, he watched what she was doing so as not to harm the little plants that seemed to be thriving despite her vigorous work. He was going to be as careful with them as he planned to be with Sapphire, because deep down he knew this was some sort of test from her.

"She's not like her sisters. She seems to have it in her head that she's not as pretty as them or as smart. She is more than they'll ever be because she's what she is." He stopped and looked at Annabelle to see if she was serious. "'Course, no man ever treated her like she was, so it's no wonder that she doesn't believe me when I tell her. You ever say that to her?"

Had he? He doubted it. Blair worked a little more before he took off his shirt and worked in his dress pants and tee-shirt. He hadn't done anything like this in a very long time, and had forgotten what it felt like to work the earth. Even the sweat trickling down his back felt good on him.

"My mother died when I was six." He had no idea why he said that, but it felt good. "I've been around men most of my life. My dad and uncles were all I had growing up because my aunts were left home to care for the children. I guess all my interaction with women was mostly my dad flirting with them and making them gush and simper. I hated it. It…I was embarrassed by him."

94

"He is a flirt, but mostly he's harmless." She moved to the next row and showed him what was planted there. "He called me just before you showed up. Then he talked to Sapphire. Don't know what they said, but she was laughing when she hung up. It was good to hear after all the crying last night and today."

Blair nodded. He'd caused her to cry all night and felt like a real shit because of it. He decided that he was going to tell her there was no more crying, then decided that would more than likely get his ass kicked. He knew these women were protective of him, and shit like that spilling from his mouth would have them all on him in two heartbeats.

"I really hurt her. I don't want to do that again." She nodded. "Annabelle, could you please help me? I want to make this up to her. I want to...I need to have her in my life. She'll be good for me."

"If she doesn't kill you. Or one of her sisters doesn't first. They're a mite pissed at you, too. Especially Emerald. That girl was nearly raised by her sister, and she's putting her through college, her and Ruby. They're going to be fine after they get out in a couple of years. Ruby will graduate this year and be a nurse like Diamond before she goes back and becomes a doctor. Emerald is gonna be a fine teacher. She loves children." She stopped working and looked up at the house, then back at him. "She's in her room. You know where it's at."

He nodded. "Does she have a gun?" When she didn't laugh, he told her he was sorry. "I don't love her, but I've grown to like her and her spirit."

"She does have plenty of that." She took the hoe from him. "A good man would go in and tell her how stupid he was. A great man would do it on his knees. A man who wants her to ever love him would beg her to forgive him and keep his mouth shut when she starts to tell you she doesn't want you, then he'd take her to bed. What sort of man are you, Blair?"

"I don't love her, as I've said. I don't know if I ever will, but I do want her in my life." She nodded and turned back to her garden. "Why are you doing this for me?"

"I'm not. I'm doing this for her." She turned her back to him, but not before he saw the tears. "You hurt her again, Blair, and I'll murder you long after I make you pay. I'm old, but I'm still as mean as a wolf protecting her cubs."

He believed her and walked over and kissed her cheek. When she moved back to her hoeing, he went to the house. It was time for him to grovel. And he was going to be the man she might love for a long time if he had to promise her whatever she wanted to forgive him. The house was silent when he made his way up the long staircase.

Chapter 9

Sapphire moaned when she felt the muscles in her back being rubbed. No one had given her a massage before, and it felt good, even if it was only a dream. When her feet were being rubbed, each toe massaged until she felt as if it was jelly, she decided that whatever she'd had before napping was going to be her choice of food from now on if it gave her dreams like this one.

"You're so tense." Blair. His voice seemed to pour over her, and she moaned again. "If you lay on your belly, I'll do your entire back."

Moving the way her dream told her, she frowned. This wasn't right. She was pissed at him. Why was she dreaming of him? Lifting her head, she looked back over her shoulder to see him straddling her and working her muscles. She flipped over so fast he nearly fell off the bed, mores the pity.

"What are you doing?" He moved to stand next to the bed and stared at her chest. She yanked the cover over her nakedness and glared at him. "I want you to leave."

"I'd like to talk to you if you don't mind." She snorted and moved to cover more of her as he sat down in her desk chair. "Please."

"I think you've said plenty. And I don't care for you right now. So if you wouldn't mind leaving, I've got work to do." He looked at the door, then back at her, but didn't move. "I mean it."

"I'm a failure." She didn't know what to say to that so didn't say a word. "I not only failed you but my father, your family, as well as anyone else that's tried to help me figure out what I'm supposed to do with you."

"Do with me?" She nearly sat up to tear into him and remembered at the last minute she was naked. "Get out."

"I didn't say that right." He stood up to pace and looked at her. "Are you completely naked under that blanket?"

"Yes. Not that it's any of your business." He nodded and paced again. "Are you leaving?"

"Will you get up and throw me out if I don't?" She shook her head. "Then no. I sort of have you captive, and I need to talk to you. It's about what I did."

"You'll have to be more specific; you've done a lot." He nodded, seemingly distracted. "Blair, will you please either sit down or get out. I've got a pounding head ache, and you're not helping. Then I have to get up and shower. I have a great deal to accomplish today, and you being here is not going to get them finished. Either say what you have to say or get the hell out."

"I'm not in love with you," he said when he sat down. "I like you well enough. I'm even beginning to have a great deal of...no, that's not right. I very much respect you. You see something you want and you simply go and get it. You don't like something or someone, you just cut them out of your life. I'm beginning to think I don't want to be cut from your life. I'd like for you to help me."

She was sure he meant it as a compliment, but for the life of her, she couldn't see it. He seemed to be hard at work on a problem, and she had the overwhelming urge to go over and comfort him. But that was simply out of the question. When he looked at her, she could see that he'd come to a monumental decision and she was going to hate it; she just knew it.

"I'd very much like to move in here with you and try to...I don't know...see if we can make it without killing each other." She knew it was going to have to do with sex and nearly told him no when he continued. "I can sleep in another part of the house if you'd like. I would love to sleep with you, but it's not the main reason I want to move in. I've been thinking of how little we see each other and we fight when we're not making love. I want to run with you too. In your back woods."

He leaned back in the chair and looked around the room. She wasn't sure this was going to be a good idea. Him living here with her sisters and grandmother would be bad. They'd kill him, and if they didn't, she most certainly would. Unless she asked them not to. Then he might survive for a week before she did it anyway. When he didn't speak for some minutes, she did.

"I have my own business now." He nodded as if he knew. "I guess Bruce told you. I've told him I'd do freelance stuff for him, but I'm not working for him. I think I'll benefit more if I don't work for either of you. I need to be in control of myself, and you two are too controlling. And if you say you're not, I will get up and knock your lights out."

"I wasn't going to. As much as I hate to admit it, I think you're right. You're brilliant as a marketer and amazing at advertising as well. Bruce went on and on about how you've saved him countless accounts and that you get the job finished quickly, too, and professionally. I'm excited to see you at work." He put his elbows on his knees and looked at her as he continued. "But this thing between us, it's not going to get any better, is it?"

"I don't think so. And I'm pretty sure that the more we try to avoid it the worse it's going to get." She looked longingly at the desk where her things were waiting for her to get started on. "I don't know what to do with you, either."

Moving in was a big step. Major because she still wanted to keep him away but knew that he was right. This thing between them was going to drive them both crazy before it was finished. But they'd either survive this or not. She thought they were both kidding each other if they thought they could be mates.

"There are four extra rooms in this house. I've taken the one next to this one as an office until I can find something downtown. You can pick and move in if my family thinks it'll be all right." She waited for him to say something, and when he only nodded, she continued. "I don't respect you, but it's only because all I've seen is how you've dealt with me and not others. Like with Bruce, I'll work some freelance for you, but you piss me off and I'll cut you off at the throat."

Blair stood up and looked down at her. She was afraid he'd get into bed with her, but she was more terrified that she'd not turn him away. When he put out his hand, she wasn't sure what he wanted, and then he smiled. She took his hand and shook it.

"I have to get back to work, but I would very much like to come back and talk with your family with you. Can I come for dinner? I want to try and convince them that I can be a nice guy, and you as well." She nodded and pulled at her hand, but he held it. "I won't disappoint you, Sapphire, or at least I'll try not to. I'll make this work. I'm not saying I won't piss you off, but I will work hard at making this work out."

When he took her hand to his mouth and kissed it, she felt her body respond. Before she could invite him in the bed or tell him to let go, he stepped back. She watched as he adjusted his cock. When he turned and left the room, she laid there for several minutes trying to get her body to calm down. The fucking man was going to kill her. And she couldn't wait for dinner tonight.

~~~

Blair made it back to his office with only having to pull over three times to take deep breaths. He kept thinking this was going to work, but then he'd think about her being naked in her bed while he was going to be living there with her. Knowing that she slept in the raw was going to be hard on him and his poor abused body.

By the time he made it to his office, he'd called his dad three times. He wanted him to go with him tonight. He wasn't sure if he'd be a help or not, but he wanted him there by his side. Plus, it didn't hurt that the women of the Erickson household liked his dad a great deal more than they liked him. His phone was ringing as he was getting his messages from Justine.

"So you're going to face the lioness are you? Are your insurance policies paid up?" He smiled at his dad's greeting. "I would say wear something you don't care about, but I hope they tear up one of your suits. Might make you seem more human if they were to see you in a pair of jeans and not a suit and tie. I know it would me."

"I'm sorry. More sorry than I've ever been about anything in my life. I should have listened to you, and more importantly, I shouldn't have been such a grade-A fuck." His dad laughed, and since he didn't hang up on him, Blair continued. "I have to go and convince the others that I'm trying. And Sapphire has said if they approve, I can move into one of the spare bedrooms and try to make this work."

"You think sleeping down the hall from your mate is going to work? I'm thinking you're going to be at each other quicker than I can say squat four times. What do you think is going to do for you beside show her what a horny bastard you are?" He flushed. "But I can see where it might help you. Being around women, especially around those women, will either teach you to respect them or they'll more than likely kill you and bury you in the back woods. Those women are strong, son. Are you sure about this?"

"No. But I have to do something. I'm afraid if I don't at least try, then...well, I don't want to go the whole rest of my life wondering if I had something great and was too pig-headed to realize it." He leaned back in his chair. "I was wondering if you'd go with me. Not to endorse me, but to sort of calm them a little if I say something stupid."

Blair didn't say he was afraid he'd say something stupid again, thinking his dad would agree with him, and he didn't want to make him mad. His dad was an amazing man, he'd just come to realize, and he wanted him beside him when he did this. He might even ignore the fact that his dad was going to embarrass him by flirting with them, but he needed him.

"I'm not saying I'll go, but what time is this thing? I got myself a date tonight, and I don't know if I want to cancel it if you're going to get us both killed." He hoped so, too. He told him what time he'd been told to be there.

"Thanks, Dad. One more thing…I want to make a better impression. What would you propose I take with me?"

His dad's laughter didn't inspire him to be confident in his answer, but when he calmed a little, his dad told him. Blair wrote it all down, and after he hung up, he looked the list over.

Wear something less stiff. He remembered that he had a pair of jeans in his closet, but wasn't sure if they were decent or not. Then he realized it was probably better if they weren't. And he knew that somewhere in the back of one of his drawers was a tee-shirt he'd worn to the gym when he had time to go, but nothing more than that. A dress shirt, maybe untucked, was going to have to do.

Take a plant for Annabelle; a tree would be great, apple. Blair asked Justine for help on that one, and she laughed all the way to her desk. He was working on his list at numbers three through five when she came back.

"What on earth do you have to take her this tree with? You can't just shove a large plant like this in a limo, and that little sports thing you drive can barely fit you, much less a good-sized tree. You know what you need? You need a truck. Go out and do something manly and purchase you a truck. You can drive one, can't you?"

He'd always wanted a big truck but had never thought them practical. But he was working on not being practical all the time and thought this was a good beginning. Blair knew nothing about them and decided that today he'd go look on his lunch hour, and added that to his list of things to do. Besides, he would need it to move his few things to Sapphire's house.

He was just getting his list covered when his dad came in to his office. He sat down as Blair was finishing up a phone call with Bruce. His dad smiled.

"I just saw Sapphire down the street. She was having a...I guess I'd call it a discussion with someone that you know. Peter Slack, remember him?" Blair nodded and picked up his jacket to go and help her out when he realized that would be just stupid on his part and sat back down. "Good boy. You might just make this work. Anyway, I made a call, and she's looking to rent her an office space. He has one right around there, and I wonder if she's thinking of renting from him. You think he'll cut her a square deal?"

"Slack would cheat his own mother if he could make a profit. And I'm pretty sure he has on occasion, too. It's why she sued him a few years back." He took a deep breath. "How do I get her to not rent from him and still be a good guy to her? Christ, this is going to be hard to stay out of her business."

"Nah, it doesn't have to be. Just ask before you leap to take over. Justine said you were going out?" He nodded. "No reason it won't take you right by her, can it? She's on the main drag last I saw her. She's probably there still. Go on out and be casual about it. Think about how much you'd like her help if'n you were trying to find something to rent. You can be subtle. I've seen you do it in meetings."

"I think I'd rather face a room full of angry clients than Sapphire on a good day. She, and no fault of hers, seems to bring out the worst in me." Blair picked up his jacket and then put it back. This wasn't a meeting he thought, but a happenchance.

Blair left the building with his dad, and when he pointed toward the car dealership down the block, Blair had his reason. He started walking and loosened his tie so that it hung askew and tried to convince himself that no one but him really cared what the hell his tie looked like. He saw her standing in front of another empty storefront that Slack owned. She turned to look at him, and he knew she was pissed off. And for once, not at him.

"He said he wants either seven grand a month or half of that if I let him fuck me once or twice on the counter." Blair felt his wolf claw at him, and he growled low. "I agree with you on that score. Too bad he's the only one that the realtor had on her list of potential leases. I don't suppose you know of anyone that has some office space to lease, do you? One that doesn't require me to fuck anyone and isn't nearly all I'll make in a year. I can't work out of my house forever, not to mention it's a little unprofessional."

"I have three buildings along this way if you're interested. You won't have to fuck me on the counter, but it would be nice." He smiled, but she only growled. "I'm teasing you, Sapphire. But as for the building…you help me with a problem I have and I'll see what we can work out on the store front."

"What sort of problem? And if you have the space in your building, I can't do that. I don't want my name associated with yours like that. People will think you've helped me out, and I can do this on my own." She looked back toward where his building was. "It would be nice digs, but I need to do this on my own."

"I understand you wanting to do this on your own. I was the same way when I started. I have other buildings. Three, as a matter of fact. And you can have your choice. What I need help with is transportation. I need a car. A truck, actually, and I know little to nothing about them. You drive one, so I was wondering if you'd help me find one that will help me move my stuff and do some of the things that I've been putting off forever." He was babbling and snapped his mouth closed when she eyed him strangely.

"You want my help?" He nodded, wondering if he should try to offer her something more, but she continued before he could think of anything. "What do you want it for besides moving your things? I'm pretty sure we can use my truck for that, if that's all you really need it for. I thought you liked riding around in your big status symbol and getting all sorts of work done while you ignored the world around you."

He was instantly pissed but tried to think what his father would say. He'd joke about being able to have other women in the back with him, but thought that wouldn't fly well with her. Blair looked at her truck parked near the curb and walked to it.

"Why do you have a truck? I mean, you could get just as much use out of something smaller, couldn't you? Plus, I was thinking that with my new pack, I'd be able to bring things to meetings. I'm not even sure what is required at pack meetings, as I've I'd never had one before." He ran his hand over the large dent in the rear panel of hers. "You didn't get hurt with this, did you?"

"No. I was teaching Emerald how to drive. What do you mean a new pack? I didn't know you had any pack, much less hauling things to it." He turned to her and smiled. She was beautiful when she was upset.

"I met with the old pack leader to challenge him, but he passed away before we could settle things. His mate took me aside and told me that if I didn't kill her I could have the entire pack and all that went with it. Did you know that as the new alpha I'm supposed to kill off the enforcer as well as the previous alpha's family if I win?" She shook her head, and he nodded. "That's what I heard later. I guess it was lucky for them that he died in a way. His son was going to kill his own mother as well as the rest of his family so that he could have a clear shot at running things his way when he took over the pack. She thanked me for stepping in."

"Grandmother met with him, the other pack leader, I mean. He told her that she would be assigned kitchen duty during the meetings. What's your view on her being at the meetings? And, for that matter, my sisters as well. Do you plan to make their lives a living hell because they're beautiful and not attached?" He wasn't sure, but he thought making a decision without all the facts would get him into hot water with her. Not that he was going to do any of those things to her family, but he did want to know what happened.

"What happened with Benetton's pack? Where did your sisters fall into that one?" She looked away, and he was afraid she wouldn't answer. "Sapphire? What happened there?"

"We didn't exactly see eye to eye with Jeffery. He wanted us to heel, and we wanted to be free. You know what happened to make us run, about him taking my sisters hostage and parading them around the meeting. He'll come for me if nothing else. I don't think he'll give up." He nodded, and she looked at the dealership. "What kind of truck do you want? And what do you plan to do with it at the house? I mean, we are always in need of a ride to somewhere. There are seven of us, not counting you, and three cars and a motorbike. I would ask that you'd be open to giving rides, please. And if moving is really all you want it for, my truck is available if one of the other cars is, or you can drop me off and use it. I trust you with her."

"Thank you for that, but as for what else, I've not a clue. I have my license, but I've not driven much over the past few years. The first time was when I drove out to your house to talk to you, and I realized how rusty I was. I like to drive, but as you pointed out earlier, I like being able to work when I'm being carted around. What do you do with yours?" They were nearly to the lot when he realized he'd not answered her question about his pack members. "Your sisters and your grandmother can be as active or inactive in the pack as they wish. I don't know how well your grandmother cooks, but I've heard from my dad that it's great, especially her apple pie. As for your sisters, like I said, whatever they want to do. Is that what you wanted to hear?"

"It's what I wanted to hear, yes, but is it the truth?" He nodded. "I guess we'll have to wait and see. I'm not saying I don't trust you, but things have a way of changing a great deal and not always for the best for us. Jeffery took a great more from us than a pack."

They spent the next two hours looking at trucks. When they test drove a particularly large and useless one, he'd made her get under the wheel and drive when he'd stalled it out twice after killing it on the open road. He wanted a stick shift, if for no other reason than she could help him get better at it.

"You're trying too hard to make it start. You have to sweet talk your car before you can expect it to perform the way you want it to." His cock felt like she'd stroked it when she continued by talking to the truck. "Come on, baby, you know you want to. Just give me a little more, and I'll ride you like a dream."

When the engine turned over, he nearly begged her to ride him. But when she turned and smiled at him, he had a feeling she had no idea what she'd done to him. They were on their way back to the dealership when his phone rang. Since he didn't recognize the number, he let it go to voicemail. But a few seconds later, Sapphire's phone rang, and he had a feeling things were about to get bad. When she looked at him as she answered, he knew it. She didn't tell him what was going on, but from her end he knew that it had something to do with Benetton.

They were walking away when she turned to him. He had declined the offer to fill out an application in deference to what she had heard. He wanted to know, but at the same time he didn't. He was afraid for her.

"Harris Benetton, Jeffery's brother, has been hurt. Badly, I'm afraid. He's at a clinic near here." She stepped closer to him to lower her voice. "The werewolf council wants me to go and see if I can help him. They're wondering if he'll make it."

"I'll come with you. If he's here in this area, then that means as alpha I should be there." He started to tell her he'd drive when he realized he was doing it again. "If you don't mind, that is. I can go later, but I'd like to have you there with me. Please."

She looked indecisive, but before he could ask her again, she nodded but had a few stipulations first. "He's a nice man stuck in a bad place. He helped us leave there, though I doubt very much if Jeffery knew it. Unless that's what he hurt him for now. I want to help him as much as I can if he asks me. You'll stay back and out of my way if he asks you to, please. If he is dying like they said, then you might make it worse if you upset him. I'm asking you, please to let me handle this."

"I understand, and I can agree to that so long as you let me help you. I'm not without the means to help you help him. All right?" He didn't think she was going to agree, but in the end, she nodded. "Good. May I ride with you then? I don't have the car with me."

"Yes, okay, but I don't like this." He knew she didn't but was glad that she'd agreed to let him go. "Harris is a good friend, and if you pull any macho bullshit on me about this mate crap, you'll be in the bed next to his."

Blair believed her. She was loyal, if nothing else, and he thought that when they were together as mates she'd be one hell of an alpha bitch for him. They were driving toward the clinic when his phone rang again. This time he answered.

"Mr. Henson, this is Andrew Mason of the Board of Weres. There's been an act of violence in another territory, and I'd like for you to have a look at the man who'd been injured. I believe he may not make it before we can get to him." The man cleared his throat twice. "His brother, Jeffery Benetton, has had a prior claim made against him. And we've set things in motion to have him removed from his position before this incident and now this. Could you see your way to—?"

"I'm on my way there now with my mate. I'll call you when we arrive. Is there anything we can do other than simply see about his wounds?"

"We have it on good authority that he is primarily a good man. He's been in a couple of issues when he was younger, but as an enforcer we've only heard good things about him. Until this. His brother is going to be dealt with, but we do worry for the safety of Harris." Blair heard papers shuffle. "We were wondering if you could see your way to invite him to your pack, even if it's only temporary. It will go a long way to helping him get better."

"I'll have to speak to my mate." Blair glanced at Sapphire as he continued. "She has vouched for his character as well, and I think will welcome him to our pack if he wishes."

"Thank you, sir. You've no idea what you've...this man Benetton, the alpha, he is a man I would not want to meet face to face when he finds out about this. He knows of the charges, but when you take him into your pack...well, there may be repercussions. Can you handle them?"

"Yes. I do believe we'll have no problems dealing with Jeffery Benetton." He looked over at Sapphire again as he finished up the call. "I do believe we'll take great pleasure in handling Jeffery Benetton."

He hung up and looked at Sapphire. "Jeffery has been a very bad alpha, and he just got the attention of the Board. I think they're having him killed. They wanted to know if we can handle him if he comes calling."

"Fuck yeah, we can handle him." She flushed. "That sounded a lot like I was looking forward to it. Trust me when I say I'm not. I'm just now healed up because of you, and I'd rather not have to deal with his sorry ass unless I have to. But I'm worried about Harris. We have to get to him before...before it's too late." Blair nodded. The truck leapt forward, and he held onto the bar over the door. When they pulled in front of the clinic ten minutes later, he was glad now that he was buying his own truck. She was a good driver, but a scary one.

Chapter 10

Jeffery watched the people coming and going in the big building. He was supposed to have been there over an hour ago, but he couldn't bring himself to go before the Board. He was going to kill Harris when he found him, then that bitch Sapphire, knowing that she had more than likely talked him into this madness.

He'd had a feeling that they were both in on a great deal that was going to shit in his life right now. And even before. Harris had been trying for months to get him to leave the Erickson women alone, and now he knew why. He'd like to have them right there before him now and show them what it meant to be hurt by him. His own brother wouldn't have done this without someone talking him into it. Harris was just too stupid to think of things on his own. When one of the younger wolves came out of the building, Jeffery stepped from behind his hiding place and smiled at him.

"Hello. I was wondering if you could tell me what all the hoopla is about. There seems to be a great many more enforcers around than normal." The pup looked around as if they made him nervous, too. "Do you know who they're looking for?"

"Yeah, some jerk-wad that hurt his brother, a Jeffery Benetton is his name. I heard that the poor enforcer won't make it, and the Board sent to some other alpha to see if they can get a handle on things before humans find out." The kid looked around and leaned closer. "I heard them saying that the guy is a rogue and will have to be put down because of this. There have been other complaints, too. More in the past few days, but all along I guess. They think they might have made a mistake in not taking him out sooner."

"Really?" Jeffery had to take a shallow breath before he could continue, his anger was so hot right now. "Do you know who would complain about this person? Maybe it was an oversight on the brother's part. Maybe he was the cause for the injury."

The kid shook his head even before Jeffery had finished speaking. "Nah, they said he hurt another alpha's bitch, too, Miss Sapphire. I met her once. She's scary. But nice. And her sisters are really nice, too. She's with the other alpha now, the one they sent to check on the enforcer. I'm thinking I might go and see if they're taking on some new members. I could always use some eye candy at the meetings. Not that I'd be able to speak to them. Those women are hot with a capital H."

So Henson and Sapphire were in on this together, Jeffery thought. He had a feeling that Henson had filed the complaint, too, the one against his mate being hurt. Well, that wasn't going to fly; he didn't even know her then. Where was the loyalty between alphas was what he wanted to know. He nearly missed what the kid was saying and looked back at him.

"They said that he's to be found and taken care of. That's what all the enforcers are doing here from other packs, to help out when he shows up for his trial. Not that I think he's coming. He was supposed to be here over an hour ago. I hope they find him soon. A guy like that should be stopped before he hurts someone else." Jeffery couldn't have agreed more.

He reached out, grabbed the kid around the throat, and jerked him twice before he heard his neck snap. Anger surged not only from Jeffery, but his wolf was pissed off, too. Moving toward the dumpster, he tossed the kid behind it as he walked by. Jeffery didn't even bother trying to hide the body, but left him hanging half out and in behind it.

The walk back to his car was made with his head down. He knew that there would be a picture of him circulating by now, and he had things to do before anyone found him. *If* they found him. He was going to make sure that if they did, he was going to go down with a great deal more than supposedly hurting some cunt that deserved it anyway. They were nothing if not exhaustive in their searches, but Jeffery had planned for such an event.

When he got into his car, he sat there trying to think what to do first. He didn't even know where they'd have his brother right now. But he knew as surely as he was sitting there that wherever he was, Sapphire would be as well, along with that fucking bastard Henson. He decided to head over to where she was living now. There had to be a clinic nearby them. He figured he had about sixteen hours to get there. And if his brother knew what was good for him, he'd better fucking be alive when he got there, too. He had things to say to the prick, and then he could have the pleasure of killing him.

Jeffery had hated the way his brother would hang around with the Ericksons when they were in the pack. Every time he needed him, he'd be there eating dinner with them or helping that old bitch in her garden. Why on earth someone would grow vegetables was beyond him. They were meat eaters for Christ's sake, not vegetarians. And no matter how many times he'd threaten him, Harris would be there. He'd even stand next to them during the moon pull. When they showed up, which wasn't all that often.

"Fucking bitches were trying to keep us apart." Which wasn't really true, but he felt he had to justify killing her, and that seemed as good a reason as any. Smiling, he thought of the night he'd tried to get his best to bring them girls to heel. He'd made sure he'd done it while Sapphire was out of town, healing after a practically bad attempt on her life. He'd just bet that Harris hadn't misjudged the man he'd sent to kill her at all, but had thwarted him on purpose. But Sapphire had returned before he'd even gotten started. And she'd hurt him, too.

Jeffery shifted on the seat when he felt one of the wounds she'd given him pull. That was another reason to kill the bitch. She'd hurt him when he'd been playing with the other girls. And it had been none of her business either. It was pack business, not Sapphire business. He wondered if she was healed yet now that she was with Henson.

His mother had told him a story once about an alpha that had injured another's mate. It had been about something stupid, too. He didn't remember the details so much as he did the end result. The female hadn't died from her injuries because she'd given herself to another alpha. They'd been true mates, his mom had told him. Like that should have mattered when the first alpha had wanted her. First come first served was his motto in things like this.

"And true mates can never be separated in life or love. Nor can they be harmed once they are mated unless the person wishes to die a horrible death. The mated pair is as one and will be until they part in this world. Harming one is like harming them both, and the remaining one will kill for their mate." He remembered thinking that having a mate had a great more advantages than not, but his mom continued. "A true mate can only be found when the fates have decided. There is only one for each of us, and if we're lucky enough to find our one, then we are a better person for it."

"Bullshit," he thought out loud. Finding a mate to fuck was all he'd ever wanted. And he'd had plenty of those. Smiling, he pulled into the gas station to fill up and to get something to eat. He smiled at the girl behind the counter.

Humans were so easy, he thought as he pissed in the sink in the bathroom, thinking about the woman out front. He marked the entire bathroom before he went back out to grab up some bags of snacks and a bottle of water. When he went up to the counter to pay, it had been on the tip of his tongue to tell her to blow him for it when a big man came from the back. He nodded once to him and left after paying up. Jeffery wasn't going to fuck with a bear, not even on his good days.

Around midnight he pulled over, put his car up on a jack, and pulled the tire off. There was nothing wrong with it, but he was a cheap fuck and actually prided himself on it. He rarely slept in a hotel when traveling if there was a wooded area nearby.

After putting the tire in the trunk and locking the car up, he slipped into the woods and stripped down. Shifting to wolf, he sat there for a long time, just waiting for the pain to recede enough to where he could move. Sapphire was going to pay for hurting his wolf.

He found a dark cave ten minutes later and was just going inside when he felt the first stir of someone trying to reach him. He waited, knowing that whoever it was wasn't a friend. Jeffery simply didn't have any. When he moved to the opening and looked around the forest, he didn't see anything out of the ordinary, but still felt uneasy. He threw back his head and howled, hoping to warn off some asshole that might be wandering around. When an answering call came back to him, he lay down and watched the forest until he couldn't hold his head up any longer. Sleep that night wasn't going to be a restful one, he thought.

Not minutes after he closed his eyes, the dreams, the nightmares, he supposed, started. Waking with a rush, he lay there very still and wondered why this one dream, and only this one, had haunted him since he'd been a teenager, and the more stressed he was, the more often the dreams would come. He had killed his mother, sure, but did the dreams of it have to make him feel like she was coming back for him?

When the sun was cresting the mountain, he went back to where he'd left his clothes and shifted again. He had to wait longer and longer after every shift until the pain eased enough for him to move. Looking down at his body, he noticed that one of the claw marks she'd given him was seeping. After touching the tender area, he put his finger to his nose and cried out. The fucking cunt had infected him somehow.

~~~

"The claw marks at his throat are what worries me the most. I have tried to stitch the wounds closed, but they simply won't heal. Unless he can get out from under the alpha that he is working for, I'm afraid that they never will. The fact that he's hung on this long amazes me. He should have died days ago." Sapphire nodded her thanks to the doctor, and when he walked away, she looked at Blair.

"Do you know what he means by getting out from under his alpha?" Blair nodded and pulled her to an empty room. She didn't fight him because she was still reeling from seeing Harris. The man looked like he'd given up and was simply waiting to die.

"It means if we take him into our pack, he'll heal. Just as you did when you and I had sex." She nodded, embarrassed by what he was telling her. "The Board has asked us to take him into our pack. I told them that I'd talk it over with you, but I'm actually going to leave this entirely up to you. You know him better than I do and can decide, and I'll back you up."

"Yes, I'd like to have him with us. I don't know what he'll do. He did say once that he had a desire to run a nursery like the one that Jade works with, but I don't know. Also, you should know that Harris told me once that he thought that Jeffery had killed their parents. I'm not sure that I don't agree with him now." She started to pace the small room. "You want to take him into your pack?"

"I...okay, I'm not sure you realize this or not, but it's *our* pack. When we were mated, the pack and all of what I have became yours." She stopped and looked at him as he continued. "And it's right on the tip of my tongue to tell you we're going to do this because it's right, but I can't. I think whatever you think about this will work, but if we have to make this decision together, then I vote we take him in or I don't think he will live."

"He's Jeffery's brother. I really like Harris, but he'd done some pretty...horrific things. The fact that he didn't like it has a lot to do with how I feel about him, but he was no less involved in some of the things Jeffery did than Jeffery was. To a point, I guess." She looked at the door, then back at him. "Will he be your enforcer, too?"

"I don't know. I've not gotten that far yet. I think he might be better served to protect you than me. You said yourself that you and he were friends, and he did have the doc call you first." She nodded at Blair. "I'm asking for your input on this, but know that one sign of trouble from him, one little hint that he isn't doing his job looking out for you, and I will drop him where he stands and not think two seconds on it."

She was flattered. She had no idea why, but the thought of him killing for her made her wolf stir, too. She knew that he'd felt her when he growled low. Sapphire watched him as he moved toward her.

"Do you want to save him?" His voice was low, rough sounding. She nodded to him, and he moved his mouth over hers gently, then down along her shoulder to the mark he'd put on her days ago. She was on fire for him, and he knew it.

"Blair, we have to go to talk to him." He growled again and set her entire body to flame. "Blair, you have to stop this."

"I know. But I can smell you." He shifted her body around so that she was flush against him. "I need to taste you, mark you again."

The knock at the door prevented her from begging him to do it, to mark her again and again and not just with his mouth. When the nurse opened the door, Blair didn't move away from her like she thought he would be, put his arm around her waist, and held her there. The nurse, a wolf too, bowed and told him she was sorry.

"The enforcer is awake now, Alpha. He is asking for the she-wolf." Sapphire tried to turn in his arms to speak to the nurse, but he held her tightly to him. She could feel his erection.

"Tell him we'll be there in one minute. We're deciding now what to do." She nodded and closed the door behind her as she left. Blair licked her shoulder again before pulling away. She stood there trembling with need as he took another, then another, step back.

"I'm not sure…this is not…I'm not sure what's going on here. I don't even know if I like it or not." He nodded and looked at the door, then back at her. "This thing between us, it's getting stronger, isn't it?"

"Yes. I can't think of anything but tossing you onto the closest hard surface and taking you all the time. Hell, I don't even care if it's hard so long as you're naked and wet for me." He rubbed his hand over his face and looked at her through his spread fingers. "Please tell me you feel this way, too. Christ, I'd really hate to think this is all one sided."

"No. I feel it as well. I don't think us living in separate parts of the same house is going to fix it either." She looked at the door before continuing. "Do you think that we can fuck it out of our systems?"

"Do you?" She shook her head. "Good, because as much as I'd love to give that a shot, I think the only thing we're going to do is be extremely exhausted all the time. We'll need to talk about it more, but now we have to help him. Do we take Harris into our pack or not?"

"Yes." She felt the rightness of it as soon as she said it. "But he's going to have to pay for his crimes. I'm not sure how just yet, but I don't think we should simply let him get by with what's happened before. And he must understand that we won't tolerate that sort of thing here. Right?"

"I agree." He put out his hand, and she thought he was going to pull her to him again, but he dropped it and smiled. "I want you. Right now I want to take you hard and fast until neither of us can move. After we talk to your family, do you think we can talk too? Then I'd very much like to shift with you and run. This has been a day from hell, and I'd like to run it off. With you beside me."

He put out his hand again, and this time she took it. When his fingers curled around her hand, she wanted to hug him to her but knew that Harris needed them right now. They entered his room to see that he'd closed his eyes. She walked to the bed and touched his face, and he opened his eye. The other one was completely closed off and swollen. Blair said his name.

"Will you serve us?" He nodded and looked at her before looking back at Blair as he continued. "You come to our pack freely? You'll pledge to us and serve us?"

"Yes." His ruined throat made his voice sound harsh and full of pain. "I will serve you for all time."

"Then I, Blair Henson, accept you as my pack member." He looked at her. "Tell him yea or nay. You'll have to accept him as well before we can help him. Accept him as my true mate."

Sapphire nodded and looked at Harris, who was staring intently at her and Blair. "I accept you into our pack. I, Sapphire Erickson Henson, accept you into our pack."

Harris's breath left his body in a rush, as if he'd been holding it for a long time and only now felt he could let it go. His entire body went lax, and she was afraid that they were too late. The monitor near his head started beeping loudly, and she looked at Blair.

"It had nearly stopped. The beeping sound—when we entered the room I noticed that the beeping had nearly stopped. It's picking up speed now. I think he's going to make it." She nodded and turned away, not wanting Blair to see her tears. But he pulled her into his arms and held her.

Fighting the tears or him was no longer an option. She sobbed against his chest for several minutes before she was able to regain control. When she tried to pull away from him, he tightened his arms around her, and she looked up at him.

"He's going to make it." She nodded. "I don't know if you'll believe this or not, but I'm falling in love with you. I don't expect you to believe me, because I've been an ass, but you're an amazing woman and I want to spend the rest of my life with you."

She wasn't sure what to say. He seemed to understand and took her hand again as they left the room. She was getting into her truck when she realized that they'd been together most of the day and hadn't fought once.

"We have to go to my house now. I have to help with dinner. Grandmother is going all out with this thing. You still want to be there, don't you?" A part of her was afraid he was going to say no, but he nodded. "Good. I think that…I know this will be hard on you. My sisters will be a little upset with you, but I think you can take it. They'll calm down after a bit."

"How many years do you suppose that will take?" She smiled at his question and started the truck. "If you wouldn't mind, I have to pick up a few things first. Most of it is at the office, but I need to go to the greenhouse on route Forty. Do you know the one?"

"Yes, Jade works there part-time." She smiled when she thought of her sisters. "Did you buy her something to butter her up? She loves daisies if you did."

"No, I bought your grandmother an apple tree. Dad said I should take flowers, but a tree he told me would be a better choice."

Sapphire thought his dad a very smart man. Grandmother loved apples and had made a pie the other day that had made Allen praise her until she'd told him to shut up. An apple tree was going to be perfect for her grandmother.

They arrived at her house just as Emerald and Ruby did. Neither of them spoke to Blair, but hugged her to them. She let them go ahead of them without saying anything. There was going to be enough yelling, she supposed, and right now they had to get dinner finished up so it could begin.

She was worried about him. She had no idea why. Her family had never really hurt anyone, but she knew that they were all protective of each other. They'd had to be over the years. Blair asked if he could help. She smiled at her grandmother when she handed him a peeler and a bag of potatoes.

"You ever peel a tater before?" He shook his head no and Sapphire was ready to do it for him when Grandmother continued. "Diamond, get over here and show this man how to work for his supper. Then when he's done I expect you all to tell him one thing about yourself. And if you don't, I will. Trust me when I tell you your story will be much nicer."

He cleared his throat after her sister gave him the rundown on a peeler and how to use it. "I was ten when my mom died. My dad wasn't much of a cook, but there were plenty of women in the neighborhood and pack that were more than willing to help us out. It's why I didn't begin this relationship with Sapphire on a good foot. I didn't want to be like him."

"Why not? He's a sweet old man." Emerald picked up another peeler and started to help him, waiting for him to answer. "When he was here last week, he helped me study for my exam. He couldn't have been nicer to me."

"You didn't see him the way I did. I guess as a kid I didn't want to be like him because of the women and not so much him. They were...simpering I guess you'd call it." Jade laughed, and he smiled at her. "I guess that's an old word, but they would come over and pinch my cheeks and tell me what a wonderful man he was. I just wanted my mom back."

Diamond sat down and started to snap peas and empty out the pods, smiling sadly at him. "I was eight when dad died. It was hard on me because I was with him when he finally just gave up on living. I never wanted him to leave us, and when we moved in with Grandmother, I wasn't a nice person. I made her life a living hell. For which now I'm very grateful that she kept me. She should have thrown me out to the streets."

"There's still time." Grandmother kissed her forehead as she walked by and put her hand on Blair's shoulder. "You should peel faster, Blair, or you'll be on kitchen clean-up duty for the rest of your life staying here."

"Yes, ma'am." Blair winked at her. "What's your story, Sapphire? Or are you going to tell me that you're much too nice to have a story that will tarnish your good name?"

He was teasing her, and she smiled. This side of Blair she liked. There were so many stories she could come up with, because she'd been a hellion as well, but she wanted something light and funny. When she thought of one, she smiled at him.

"When I was in ninth grade, I decided to go to the junior prom as a wolf. I don't have any idea why at the time it seemed like it would work, but it didn't even come close. It resembled a scene from the movie *Carrie* where all the people came rushing out of the building and blood was everywhere. Not because of me, but because they kept tripping up on those ridiculous dresses and heels they wore. Grandmother grounded me for six months of no social activities, and I had to wear a dress and heels the entire time. That was more painful than the social stuff."

They all laughed, and Blair winked at her. She felt good and for the rest of the dinner prep and dinner itself they told stories, as well as laughed. She was sorry to see it end when it did.

Five hours later, the two of them were in the kitchen loading the dishwasher when her sisters came in. She looked at them, and then at Blair. He walked behind her and reached for her hand. Sapphire had asked them if he could move in, to see if they could make this work during dinner. It looked like they'd come to a decision. She'd never been so afraid in all her life. Ruby pulled out a sheet of paper.

"He can stay, but there are going to be rules. Rules that can't be broken no matter what." Blair nodded, and she felt him squeeze her fingers. "Rule one: you have to put the toilet seat down. You're the only male in this house, and you'll abide by our peeing, not yours."

"I can do that." She winked at him, and when she looked down at her list, he interrupted her. "I'll do whatever it takes, I swear to you. I'll sign in blood to any of those rules so long as you'll give me a chance."

"Will you buy tampons for us if you're in town and we're having an emergency?" He nodded at Emerald. "Then he's fine with me. Let's have some pie. I'm hungry again."

And just like that, Blair Henson had a new address.

Chapter 11

He was running late. Again. Blair had never had to share a bathroom so much in all his life, and this house had a great many of them, too. He'd also discovered over the past five days that he didn't care for oatmeal no matter how you dressed it up with sugar and butter, and he wasn't going to survive without coffee. Tea wasn't cutting it. He looked over at Emerald, who'd asked for a ride to college with him.

"I need coffee." She smiled at him and directed him to a Tim Horton's. "Thank God. I like the tea we have at dinner, but I need a caffeine hit this early. How do you study all night and look like you've had nine hours of sleep instead of the nine minutes I think you actually had?"

He knew she was studying hard for her finals in two weeks, and everyone in the house had been assigned time with her to help out. She leaned her head back and closed her eyes.

"I'm worried about you." He glanced at her as he got onto the highway. "You do know that there are more than enough bathrooms for us to use without making you late every morning, don't you?"

He'd figured that out last night. Every time he went into one of them, someone would knock. He decided to pay them back today. He smiled when he thought of his plan. He only hoped it didn't backfire on him. They were a vicious group when they wanted to be.

He changed the subject. "I need your help with something. I have this client coming into the office today who is looking for a fresh idea for his product. It's an old idea with a twist. He wants to market his veggie trays with a dip to hit the younger crowd."

"Sapphire and I were talking about that a few weeks ago. She had this great idea that there should be a larger container with smaller ones that would fit inside of it. Sort of a 'pick what you want' thingy. Then a few dips besides just ranch or dill. I personally like salsa with my veggies, but I don't like broccoli."

He could see it now. He looked at her when she didn't say anything else and realized she was asleep. Blair pressed a button in his steering wheel and said Sapphire's name to call her. It was the greatest thing he'd gotten on his new truck.

"I need you for some work today. Can you spare about two hours and come to my office? I have a client that might like your vegetable tray idea that Emerald was telling me about." She didn't say anything for a few seconds, and he was worried. "Love?"

"Okay, but what time? I have a client coming in today, too, and that person I hired to help me with the phones quit already. She said I was stifling her creative muse. I asked her not to paint her nails on my time. How is that stifling her?" Blair laughed, and she huffed at him. "I don't have time to interview a person again. This process is…it's stifling my ability at making any money."

"You help me out today, and I'll send you someone that you can use until you find a replacement. I don't think she has much of a creative muse, but she might. What do you think?" She didn't say anything. "And I'll let you take me to lunch."

"Gee, how incredibly nice of me. How could I refuse?" He smiled. "I'm on my way to the office now. How soon do you need me? And I can't be there until someone comes here. I can't let the phones just ring again today."

"I'll call as soon as we get off of here and have Tanya go over. It's not that far, so she might be there when you get there. She's a human. Do you have a problem with that?"

"I don't care if she'd a bird so long as she can work for me." He heard her sigh. "Blair, I want this to work, but I'm running into more obstacles than I am solutions. And one client isn't going to pay the rent." He knew that she didn't have to worry about that, but no amount of telling her that was working.

"I'm nearly to the university so I'm going to lose you. I have this guy coming in at nine-thirty. Can you be here at nine? The sooner the better." He pulled onto the lot just as Emerald was waking up. "I'll see you soon."

"I'll be there. I have some work done up on it, but I'll have to find it. I'm about ten minutes from my office now." He left the lot after making sure that her sister had enough money to eat. He'd never seen anyone put away as much food as she did and still remain as thin as she was. He laughed when Sapphire told her sister via the connection to stay out of trouble.

He called the office and asked to have Tanya Martin sent over to Sapphire's office. He was nearly to the office when he heard back from Sapphire. She sounded thrilled.

"I love her. And you may or may not get her back. She's already set me up two appointments for this week and has sent them to my calendar. I love someone who will work with me."

"She's been making noises about leaving the firm. Something about an office romance gone bad. Maybe if you still like her by the end of the week, you and she can work something out." Blair pulled into his parking space as he continued and switched his phone to his ear piece. "Are we still on for lunch then?"

"Yes if you don't mind driving. I want to try that new gyro place down from the mall. Do you have time to go that far?" He'd go to the end of the world for her if she wanted him to. "We can do closer if you don't have the time."

"That sounds perfect. We should be finished here around then, so we'll leave from here. I don't think I have another appointment until three or so." And if he did, then he'd just reschedule. "I'll expect you soon then?"

"I'm leaving here in ten minutes. I found the mock-ups and the little containers that I made up to have a visual. I hope this firm is seriously opened minded. I'm not much of an artist when it comes to food."

"I'm sure it'll be fine." He ended the call just as he was going into his office. He pulled up his calendar to see what he had going after lunch and saw that the whole day had been cleared for Thad Galloway of Galloway Industries.

Blair leaned back in his chair to wait for Sapphire. He thought about the past week with her and her sisters and realized how much more he wanted. Sapphire was everything he never realized he'd wanted in a female, much less a mate.

He thought about using her bathroom last night. It had smelled like her, and he'd nearly gone to find her to see if the shampoo on the little shelf was what her hair smelled like. And her skin was as soft as the bottle of body soap said it would be. Christ, he missed touching her. He found himself trying to find reasons to brush against her, touch her when she handed him something or passed him a bowl at dinner. She was driving him insane.

He supposed insane was a mild word for what she was doing to him, and he was depressed to think that he wasn't having the same effect on her. She seemed to be oblivious to him and what she was doing to him simply by being herself. When he looked in the doorway, he saw her standing there, and he suddenly needed to not just touch her, but to taste her as well. Standing slowly, he moved toward her.

"You should probably know that they gave me a badge downstairs that is mine. Your security personnel said that it would save me time." He nodded at her, not really having a clue what she was talking about, nor caring for that matter. "I think they need to take a better picture of me because this one is a little…a little…what are you doing, Blair?"

"Touching you." He ran his fingers down her arm and up again. "Do you know how delicious you smell right now? Like a field after the rain has come through."

He touched his mouth to hers, pulled her out of the doorway, and closed it behind her. She went into his arms willingly, and he felt his heart rate pick up. When she moaned, he took a step toward the door and pressed her against it. Christ, she fit him like a warm glove.

He wanted to tell her he wanted her, but couldn't tear his mouth from hers. Her tongue moved with his until he couldn't tell whose was whose. Lifting her leg up, he wrapped it over his hip and rocked into her warm flesh and looked down at her.

Her lips were swollen from his mouth, her breasts were heaving, and he could see her nipples as they poked against the silk of her blouse. Blair ran his thumb over the hard peak and watched her face. Sapphire cupped his hand over her and held him there.

"I can't stand this. All I think about is you and sex." He was shocked by her admission, but before he could tell her he felt the same way, she rocked into him. "Blair, do you have any idea what you're doing to me?"

"Yes. Christ, you're making me feel the same things." Picking her other leg up, he took her throat when she wrapped her ankles around him. "I want to be inside of you in the worst possible way."

"Please," she begged him, and he moved them toward the couch. Laying her back on it, he moved over her just as someone knocked on his door. Sapphire growled low and he couldn't have agreed more.

"We're having a meeting right now." She looked at him with eyes that were glazed and needy looking. "Sapphire, I don't want to stop this either, but Justine will only continue knocking until we open the door."

As if she heard him, she knocked again. This time was harder, and they both heard her giggle. Blair was going to kill her if she said one word to him. Lifting his body from Sapphire's, he kissed her hard and took a step back. He wanted to help her adjust her clothing, but he had a feeling he'd be removing it rather than making her look presentable. She glared at him when he reached for her again. He dropped his hands from just reaching to run them through her hair again. Christ oh mighty, she looked deliciously tousled.

"You're going to have to do something with your hair. I'm afraid that I mussed you a bit." He pointed to his personal bathroom, and when she stepped around him, he did pull her to him and kissed her again. "Just so you know, lunch is out of the question. I'm going to be hard pressed to make it through this meeting without taking you on the table."

She walked around him, giving him a wide berth. It might have been funny if he didn't blame her for it. He tried to calm both his wolf and his cock. Both of them were aching for the woman, and he tried to take several deep breaths when Justine knocked again. He opened the door just as Sapphire came out of the bathroom looking as fresh as she'd looked when he'd first touched her. She smiled at Justine and took the hand of Thad. He was smiling and Blair wondered what Justine had told him about them. When he winked at them, he knew. Damn it, he was embarrassed for some reason.

"Hello, beautiful." Thad kissed Sapphire's hand, and Blair had to tell his wolf that the man was human and had no idea that he was poking the bear, so to speak. "I heard great things about your company."

"It's not my company, but Blair's. I just do some freelance work with him and a few other companies. We've worked well together on this project for you." Sapphire led him to the table just as Justine brought in a large box and another of his staffers brought in some long tubes that art was generally stored in. Blair watched her do what he was sure was a gift. She would make this work, and he was sure that the client would never know it was only a concept until an hour ago.

~~~

She was nervous. Sapphire was looking at the deal of her life, and it wasn't the client she was thinking about. When she and Blair came together, and there was no doubt in her mind that they would, it would be forever. She glanced at him when Thad picked up her mock-up of the container. Blair was looking at her as if she were a tasty morsel of steak.

"How much would you think something like this would go for?" She had to drag her eyes from Blair to look at Thad. "Do you think this would be something that would be a toss-away? Or were you proposing something more?"

"More. The larger tray would be something that they could purchase once and then refill with different products every day if they wanted. I thought of colors, too, for children's lunch boxes, as well as some that you could offer with licensing logo, such as football teams or even local high school. It would be expensive if you didn't have your own in-house artist, but I think in the long run you'll be a major contender in this. People are trying to eat smarter. You're going to be offering them a way to eat what they want in a container that can also save on the environment." She picked up the smaller container and dropped it into the larger one in his hand. "The way you make the four or six blocks can invite a great many things. Colors for instance. Veggies in green, fruit in red, and even some of the more popular dips in a cream or white. Don't make the smaller ones reusable for the simple fact that people will, and you're here to make a profit."

He sat there for several minutes playing with the different combinations. She'd brought her containers filled with carrots and celery so he could see what she meant. When a small touch to her mind stirred, she felt a shiver over her body like she'd been touched.

I've forgotten about our link. I've only ever used it with my dad, and never thought about the fact that you and I have one. She felt his touch as if he'd actually done it. *I'm going to give you a fat bonus if he goes for this deal. What would you like?*

You, came from her mind uninhibited. *I want you. I've never...well you know that I've never wanted anyone before, but when you touch me, fill me, it's all I can do not to scream.*

I want you to scream. I want you to come so hard when I'm inside of you that you hurt from it. She nodded without thinking. *He's talking to you, love. Perhaps we should table this for later.*

"Are you all right?" She looked at her client and smiled. "You sort of spaced out there for a second. Tell me you have more ideas like this one. Ones that will continue to make me look environmentally sound and clear a profit as well?"

"Yes. I have a great many food ideas. I have five sisters, and we're all watching our weight all the time." They weren't, but he didn't have to know that. "Did you know that your drink containers could use a new look? They're just like most of the others on the market. If you made them in a different shape, they'd fit in coolers easier, as well as children's lunch boxes. Round doesn't fit well when sandwiches as well as most containers are square, too."

Thad stood up and turned to Blair, who she just realized had said very little since she'd taken over. She'd have to apologize to him about that. She'd not meant to shove him out of the way like she had.

"You keeping her on staff?" Blair nodded at his client. "Good. I would like to have us go into business together. You will be our only marketer for say the...I'm thinking forever, but I'm not going to harm either of us on that score, but I would like to have the next ten years of your undivided attention. So long as she stays on staff. I like her."

"I think we can arrange that. I'm in love with her." She looked at Blair as he made that announcement. "Of course, I have to convince her that she loves me, but I think we can work together well until she realizes how much I need her in my life."

Thad nodded and smiled. "You're a lucky man. I'll have my attorneys call yours. I'd like to see production started on this as soon as we can get it rolling. I'll also need a fresh logo as you pointed out. Something that reflects the times and move from my father's era."

They set an appointment for her to go to his main offices next week and for Blair to go to the production end. The two of them were going to be spending a week in Texas where the main office of Galloway Industries was located very soon to get this ball rolling. Holy hell, she'd gotten her first major client. When he left, she started to gather up her things when she felt Blair's arm snake around her waist.

"You just made us very rich, and we're only going to get richer if this keeps up." She nodded as he moved her hair from her shoulder. "I'm in the mood to have a feast. What would you say if I asked you to lie across this table and let me drink from you?"

She turned in his arms, wrapped her arms around his shoulder, and held him to her. "You said I could scream. I want to do that and so much more. I want to hear you howl again when you come inside of me. Then I want to run with you in the wood so you can take me again. What do you think of that?"

He kissed her hard and with hunger. She gave him as well as she got, and when he lifted her ass up and pressed his cock into her, she moaned. When he lifted his head she could see his wolf just on the surface. Her own wolf growled at her.

"Where? And please tell me it's closer than your home." She shook her head and licked his pounding pulse. "We're not going anywhere unless you stop now."

"I think we should go home. Grandmother is going to her friend's house for the day, and the others are at work or school. I can make it worth your while if we—" He was dragging her to the elevators, and she giggled.

While they waited on the doors to open, he barked at Justine that he was finished for the day and not to call him. The woman laughed as they stepped into the elevator as soon as the door swished open. Blair had her pressed against the wall before the doors were completely closed. They were not going to make it to the house before they came all over each other.

Chapter 12

"What do you mean you've gone with another pack?" Jeffery and his brother were standing outside the courtroom that was to hold his retrial, and Harris wasn't making any sense. "You can't just do that. I'm your fucking brother."

"You are, but you're a prick and an asshole, and I've not wanted to be a member of your pack since you took over. You're mean, vindictive, and you aren't a good leader. But that's not all, I simply don't like you." Harris looked around before continuing. "I hope things go badly for you today, Jeffery. I sincerely do."

"Why?" This was making no sense to him. Jeffery had been a leader like he thought his father had been. The fact that Harris didn't like him didn't bother him overly much, because if he was truthful he didn't care for him either. But to leave him for another pack simply wasn't right.

"Why? You nearly killed me, you motherfucker. You tore at my throat as if I was nothing to you. And the fact that you have to ask me why just confirms what I've heard about you. You're a heartless bastard." Jeffery snorted at his brother as he continued. "I'm not going to lie about anything they ask me in there. Nothing. I plan to tell them everything you had me do. I'll be damned if I'll cover for you again."

"You're acting like you gave me a choice in harming you. You're not dead, are you? You seemed to be healed just fine. That has to count for something." Jeffery tried to think about all the things his brother knew about him and was scared. "You wouldn't want me to lose my entire pack over you pissing me off, now would you? Christ, Harris, I was just funning with you."

Harris walked away. Before he could reach for him to tell him...no, order him to drop this entire silliness, he saw his lawyer coming toward him. He'd hired the guy from the phone book because he'd had the biggest ad in the monthly newsletter the Board sent out. He had no idea what, if any, experience he had in pack law.

"Mr. Benetton, you should have told me that your brother was no longer a member of your pack. This makes things a great deal more...difficult for you." He handed him a file. "And according to the information I was given just this morning, it looks as if you need more of a criminal lawyer instead of one for a simple misunderstanding between you and the Board."

Jeffery fanned out the information in the file and saw that his brother had already talked. Mother fuck, he'd even given dates as well as information on where he'd hidden the bodies at his command. He looked up at the lawyer, completely forgetting if he ever knew his name.

"He did these things. Why am I on trial for them?" The lawyer took the file back and slipped it into his brief case. "How can I be responsible for his actions? I'm just the alpha, not his keeper."

"You're both, in the event you didn't know that. Once you become alpha of a pack, you assume all responsibility to the people you govern. That includes your enforcer. And, for your information, he has tapes of conversations between the two of you, all done legally because you signed a waiver to him several years ago. Why the hell wasn't that in your disclosure to me?" He handed Jeffery two sheets of paper that had little tabs on them. "The second page clearly is your signature. You gave him the rights to record all conversations as well as record video of the two of you whenever you were together. I don't think your brother ever trusted you."

Jeffery staggered back from him. He remembered this now. He'd just confessed to his brother how he'd murdered their father. And Harris had pulled out this paper as well as his phone. He'd even recorded him signing the stupid thing. He looked at the man standing before him.

"I'm not going to lose my pack over this. How on earth will I ever be able to show my face at the pack meetings from now on with this on my record?" The lawyer just stared at him as he tried to wrap his mind around this. "Can you fix it so I can remain alpha? I'll try to be good from now on."

No, he wouldn't, and they both knew it. His first order of business was to kill Harris, then piss on his motherfucking body. The lawyer wasn't finished, it seemed, and handed him another file. This one was thick, and Jeffery didn't even bother opening it. If all he was going to give him was bad news, he didn't want him to represent him any longer.

"You should know that as of now I'm not your attorney. I've been asked to step aside by the Board because of reasons only they know. I think it's because you're a prick and they thought I could do better. As for you not losing your pack over this? That's a done deal. What you should be worried about is how long you're going to be in prison for all that you've done." The man started to walk away but turned after only a few steps. "Do you have a gun, Mr. Benetton?"

"Yes, of course I do. I have to have protection from idiots now that my enforcer has decided to leave me in an unguarded position. I can't be expected to be defenseless. You know what sort of people are out there." He laughed at him, and Jeffery took a step toward him when the lawyer spoke again.

"Please do. I'd very much like for you to try and attack me." He laughed again. "I'd put that gun to my head if I were you. Once everything comes out, and it will, you're going to be lucky someone doesn't murder you slowly and show you as little mercy as you showed most of the people who looked to you for leadership. Help you keep your pack? I just hope to Christ they tear you apart for your crimes before you are sentenced."

He moved out of the building, and Jeffery stood there for several minutes, thinking. His list of crimes was long. Just in the past year he knew that if anyone found out, he'd be strapped up and poison poured through his body, if they did that to his kind. He moved slowly toward the door, thinking he had to leave now or he'd never get another chance. He was stepping through the opening when he heard his name being called. He was so fucked if they caught him.

He slipped into his beater. He'd purchased this thing just after he had gotten out of high school. Jeffery had only kept it because it was something he would go out to the garage and look at when he was feeling particularly put out about some grievance someone had brought to his attention. Was he really expected to solve all their problems? He thought his pack thought that. Jeffery glanced in the back seat.

There were clothes in suitcases as well as an entire one filled with cash. Skimming the dues he'd instilled against his pack members had been right there for the taking, and he did. Jeffery smiled as he pulled into traffic and headed in the opposite direction of his house and the building of the Board. He had to make tracks if he was leaving town in one piece. He'd show the motherfuckers.

As he stopped at the light just past Main Street, he saw them…both Sapphire and Henson coming out of a huge building right in front of him and walking to a parking garage not fifty feet from him. Looking at the building closely, he saw the name *Flair Marketing* and knew the name. She was working for him. Then he saw them kiss.

The passion there made his skin heat and his body flush with their apparent need for each other. He watched as Henson touched her, touched what was his, and she didn't fight back. When her arms wrapped around him, Jeffery knew hatred, a fury so hot and heavy that he nearly got out of the car to go and kill them both. He even had his hand on his door mechanism, ready to leap at their throats, when a horn from the car behind him blared, reminding him where he was and that there were entirely too many witnesses to do what he knew he had to. They had to die.

Jeffery moved forward under the light and into the next street. By the time he got back around to where he'd seen them, they were, of course, gone. He pulled into the same lot and asked about Henson, but the young woman at the booth told him that she couldn't give out that sort of information. When he snarled at her, she simply pressed a button on her counter and all the windows turned dark, and he realized that she'd blocked him out. And no amount of pounding on the windows would make her come out, either. Jeffery got back into his car and drove to the first hotel, a cheap one, and got himself a room. He was glad now he'd seen a program on finding other identities and had spent the extra cash to make him into a whole new person.

He took out the phone book and started looking for Erickson's when he realized how old the book was. Ten years ago Sapphire had been a kid and not living in this town. He tossed the useless book across the room and lay back on the bed.

He had to find her. Then he was going to make her pay, and by pay, he meant she was going to fucking die. She hadn't caused all his problems, but she'd been a big part in the fact that he was now in trouble with the board. If only she'd kept her fucking mouth shut when he'd told her to. And his brother, too.

Harris had actually gone to another pack. How was that even possible? Jeffery sat up suddenly. He'd not just gone to another pack, but to Henson's pack.

"Mother fuck. This is not happening to me. This is fucking not happening to me. First, Sapphire gets away with mistreating me, and now this. Oh this is not going to end well for Henson or Sapphire. No sir, it is not going to end well at all for either of their fucking asses."

He had to find them, and since he couldn't go to the Board and ask them where the new pack leader was, he had to...the phone ringing startled him. He'd not given the number to anyone and had no idea who would be calling him. He picked it up cautiously, trying his best to remember what his fake name had been. Lucky for him, the man at the other end cleared that right up.

"Mr. Wright? This is the front desk. Could you please come to the office? There seems to be a problem with your credit card. It's been reported as lost or stolen." He heard the man talk to someone else. "We'll need you to bring cash to pay for the room if you wouldn't mind. Now would be better than later."

"Sure. I'll get right on that." He hung up and was glad now that he'd not brought any of his things inside. Going out to his car, he got in and moved out of the lot. He would have to use cash from now on, he supposed, and went to find another hotel.

~~~

Blair turned off his truck. They both looked at the house as they sat there. He wanted to ask her if she'd changed her mind but was sort of afraid of the answer. When she turned to him and smiled, he thought he could conquer the world.

"Do you think we could run first? I've not been in a few days and find that it relaxes me. I'm sort of tense." She opened her door before he could answer her and walked to the front of his truck. While she stared at him, she began unbuttoning her blouse. He didn't move.

When she slipped if off her shoulder and it slid to the ground, Blair felt his cock stretch and fill. She cupped her breasts and tilted her head back. The long column of her throat beckoned him, and he began to unbutton his own shirt. Her bra slid up and over her and exposed her hard, pink nipples. He was out of the truck before he could think about it.

"Don't touch me yet. I want to strip slowly for you, and you'll rush me." He stepped back to allow her room to do whatever she wanted. "I've never wanted to be naked for a man before. I find the fact that you're not touching me yet very erotic."

"You have no idea what this is doing to me." She cupped his cock, and his breath swooshed out of him. "Christ, you're going to kill me."

"I want to suck your cock. I don't want you to come yet, but I do want to taste you." He nodded because he was sure he'd lost all feeling in his head, and speech was impossible. "Will you tell me if I do it wrong?"

He nodded again and put his hand on the hood of the truck when she dropped to her knees. He watched as she removed her bra and had to turn slightly to lean against something or fall. Blair was sure that when she touched him, whether she wanted him to come or not, he was going to.

He'd left his jacket at work, and his tie had come untied at some point in the morning. He reached up with trembling hands and pulled it free of his shirt and finished unbuttoning it. She opened his belt and left it hanging, and he nearly fell back when she opened the zipper with her teeth.

"Sapphire, please don't tease me much more. You've no idea how hard this is on me." She smiled at him and pulled his pants down around his thighs, along with his boxers. Rubbing her cheek over his length, he nearly tore his shirt in half, trying to get lose from it. His cock seemed to leap at her.

Blair wanted to beg her to touch him, but he wanted her to take her time. He watched as she stared at his cock for several seconds before her tongue came out and licked the very tip. He saw stars. And when she wrapped her mouth around his crown, Blair cried out suddenly. Christ, her mouth was hot.

Fucking her luscious mouth as gently as he could, Blair curled his fingers into the back of her head and held her to him. Her tongue danced along his cock with every movement, and every time he was ready to explode into her, she'd move. When she cupped his balls and leaned back, he was on the verge of snarling at her to finish him when he looked at her. There couldn't have been a more beautiful woman in the world than her.

"I want you to fuck me." She stood up, and he reached for her. "No, as a wolf. I want him to fuck me, take me hard and fast. Then I want you to take me, too, right out there in the forest. Can you...please?"

She tore at her skirt, and the material joined his shirt in the grass when her panties came off. She shifted so quickly he had a moment to wonder at it. But she took off, and he let his own wolf take him, tearing his pants from his human self as he disappeared. He caught her scent just as he entered the darkened area.

Her scent was everywhere because these were her woods. Blair had to concentrate hard on finding the freshest one, and when he found it, he moved after her. She seemed to be everywhere. When she jumped out from under a bush, it was all he could do not to run after her immediately. He wanted to chase her, hunt her down, and take her on his own. So he let her run again. He was going to enjoy this.

He found her ten minutes later. The game had gotten frustrating for him, but he was determined that he would get his prey. When he saw her move, he slid up behind her and bit deeply into her shoulder until she lay still. She snarled at him twice before he moved over her.

Nothing in the world could have prepared him for the feeling of entering his mate this way. His cock seemed to fill almost immediately, and when she lifted her hind quarters up for him, he let go of her shoulder long enough to cover her. Planting his paws over her shoulders to lower her, she did as he directed her.

He wants to mark you. Her wolf snarled at him, but Sapphire laughed. *You won't think this is so funny when he bites you. He will scar you.*

I'm going to scar him too when he's finished. I want the world to know that you belong to me. He started moving in and out of her, and she moaned through his mind. *Harder, she wants it harder.*

He didn't want to deny his mate or her wolf. His body slammed into hers. He didn't want to hurt her, but he also didn't know if he could stop. When she tightened around him, Blair knew his wolf wanted to tear into her muscles, and no amount of begging him to be careful would slow him. As soon his wolf bit down into her shoulder, he came with a roar against her, and his balls emptied. She howled. Blood filled his mouth as he came inside of her.

The wolf held her down while he licked the wound closed. As soon as he shifted slightly to allow her to move, she flipped him off her and stood over him. His wolf was not happy with the turn of events, but before he could knock her back, Sapphire's wolf leapt at him and bit hard into his shoulder.

His beast stilled. Blair wasn't sure if he was gearing up for an attack on her or he liked her biting him back. When her head tore at him, he felt the pain of the mark burn into his flesh and waited for her to finish. When she licked the wound closed and moved back, his wolf stayed where he was.

Her human came over the she-wolf in degrees this time. Slowly, the fur receded, and skin and muscle appeared by the time she was fully human Blair knew what his wolf wanted. He wanted to taste the human, too.

Moving forward, she didn't try to stop him but spread her legs for him. The wolf, his wolf, gently licked at her thigh, then up over her hip. When she moaned, his wolf moved his muzzle to her wet curls and licked. Her body shuddered, and his wolf drank deeply.

Come for him. Blair watched her body seem to bow, and when the wolf licked her clit, she came apart screaming out his name and holding his wolf to her. When he stepped back, Sapphire crumbled to the ground, and Blair shifted. It was his turn.

He wanted to drink from her as well. Wanted to taste himself on her, but his need to fuck her overwhelmed him. Nearly tossing her to her back, he opened her legs wide and looked down. She was soaking wet, and he couldn't wait any longer.

Fisting his cock, he held it at her entrance as he watched her. Sapphire was watching him, and he entered her hard. As soon as his cock was to the root, she wrapped her legs round his waist and her arms around his shoulders. Christ, he was as deep as he'd ever been in a woman.

"Hard. Fuck me hard and fill me." He cupped her ass and brought her as tightly against him as he could and rocked his hips. Every time he moved into her, she'd beg him for more. As soon as his balls tightened against his body, he licked her shoulder in the place where his wolf had bit, and sank his teeth into her.

Sapphire screamed as she came around him. She had him wrapped so tightly inside of her that he almost couldn't move. When she sank her own teeth into his scar, he came. His entire body seemed to shatter, coming apart in a storm of pieces, only to come back to him. He dropped over her even as her body continued to tremor around him.

Blair lifted his head to look down at her. Her eyes were closed, and her body was lax beneath his. Smiling, he started to move off her when she put her arms around him.

"I love you." Blair stilled at her words. "I think I have for a long time but didn't want to."

"Sapphire?" She smiled, and her arms went limp, dropping to the ground. "I love you too, darling. I love you with all my heart."

Blair held her to his body. She loved him was all he could think about. Sapphire loved him, and he loved her. Everything was going to be all right.

Chapter 13

Pulling into the drive after fighting with the traffic, Annabelle was exhausted. She thought of going inside and simply letting the things stay in the car, but knew she wouldn't do it. First of all, there were frozen things in the bags, and she wasn't going to enjoy a bath knowing she'd not finished a job. Getting out, she noticed something seemingly leaping across the yard. When she went to pick it up, she was dismayed to find it was one of Sapphire's blouses. Then she found a pair of Blair's shoes. Laughter burbled from her mouth when she realized what had happened and looked out toward the woods.

She picked them all up and was ready to toss them into the trash when she thought of using them. She had no idea why a baby's blanket came to mind to use the scraps for, but she started cutting out the tiny squares as soon as she put on a roast for dinner after bringing in all the bags. She had a bounce in her step, she noticed, that hadn't been there before. She was nearly finished with Sapphire's things when the phone rang.

"I was looking for my son. We were to meet at the bank an hour ago, and he's not answering his phone." Poor man had sounded so mad she nearly laughed.

"I think he and Sapphire have come to terms with their being mates. I just picked up their clothing that was blowing all over the yard. I think they're in the woods." He was quiet, and she thought she'd lost him when he spoke.

"They really are? I mean, you think that they've finally gotten over this aversion and are now going to make us some grandbabies?" He sounded so hopeful that she smiled. "Christ, if he asks, tell him I'll take care of the loan. Tell him...tell him.... I have no idea what to tell him. I love him is all I can think of."

"I'm sure he'll be happy to hear it." She looked out the window to the woods and thought of something. "Oh my, they won't be able to come inside now that I'm here. I'll put them out some clothes. Why don't you come for dinner tonight and we'll congratulate them together? Hopefully they'll come down for food sometime."

"I'll be there. With bells on." She heard his laughter. "Hot damn, I've a new family. More daughters than a man could hope for."

After they hung up, she found some of Blair's clothing in the laundry room as well as some things of Sapphire's. She set them out on the deck railing and closed the door behind her. She wanted to watch to see when they came to get them, but knew it would embarrass not only them but her as well. She set up the ingredients to bake a few pies.

Two hours later, she was pulling the first of three pies out of the oven when the door behind her opened. She didn't bother turning, thinking it was the kids. Smiling, she set the apple pie on the cooling rack.

"I was beginning to wonder if you were going to stay out there all day." When neither of them answered, she turned and saw Jeffery standing in the doorway. "What are you doing here?"

"I've come to kill Sapphire and Henson. Where are they?" She didn't look out to the woods as he continued. "She's fucked around long enough that now she has to die instead of just being punished. She's not a good she-wolf."

"What she did to you, you deserved. More if you asked me." She moved her body toward the block of knives, but he stopped her.

"Move again and I'll tear your throat out. I'm not here for you, but if you fuck with me, I'll kill you just as easily." She felt her wolf stir, and he took a step back from her. "You shift, old woman, and you'll be dead before you can become wolf. I promise you that."

"You're a bastard, and we're well rid of you." The fist came out quickly and slammed against her mouth hard enough to knock her off her feet. She didn't get up but watched him pace. Annabelle reached for Sapphire.

Jeffery is in the house. You have to stay away because he's crazy pissed off at you and Blair. I can handle him.

I'm on my way; so is Blair. Don't you dare take him on, Grandmother, or so help me, I'll be really pissed myself. Annabelle knew that when Blair got to Jeffery he was going to be a dead man.

"They're coming now. Both of them." He stopped pacing and stared at her. "I've contacted them, and they're on their way."

"What hotel did they go to after they left his office?" She frowned at him, not understanding. "I saw them today. Out on the street in front of his office. All lovey-dovey that it made me want to puke. When will they be here?"

She saw the big wolf out of the corner of her eye but didn't say anything. She knew it was Blair and was taken aback at his size. He was twice the wolf that Jeffery had ever been, and she was actually somewhat afraid of him. When he moved into the room with them as quietly as a mouse, she looked at Jeffery again.

"You should really learn to understand defeat. When Blair attacks you, he is going to kill you. I've no doubt about that whatsoever." Jeffery snorted, and she saw Blair sit. "Why are you doing this? What on earth do you hope to gain by harming either of them? Or me for that matter."

"Harming you is a bonus. The other two I'm doing simply for the pleasure of it. And pay back. He's taken my pack from me, did you know that? Even my own fucking brother left me for that fucking prick. Why, I ask you? What on earth does he have that I didn't have?" When Jeffery sat down, she could see the gun in the front of his pants and could barely focus on his words, much less him. "Harris turned me in. He actually had the nerve to tell them that I'd hurt him."

"Did you?" He grinned and nodded. "Then what are you so upset about? If you hurt him, he had full right to turn you in to the Board. What did you expect him to do?"

"Be loyal. Respect my position as his alpha and brother. I don't think that's too much to hope for from your own brother, do you?" She didn't answer him. "Anyway, he's healed up now. What does it matter?"

She felt Sapphire touch her mind. *Keep him talking. The Board is on their way. Blair said that if he touches you, he'll kill him, but he doesn't want you hurt in the process. The people at the Were office are better able to handle this for now.* She felt her love. *I do love you, Grandmother.*

More than I've ever loved anyone before. And I love Blair as well.

Well, of course, you do. Why would you not? Annabelle looked at Jeffery as she continued with her granddaughter. *He's insane. I don't mean that in a smart-alecky way, but I really think he's off his noodle.*

He is. That's another reason we need to call the Board. The wolves that work there are a force that will make sure he gets the help he needs. She looked up when Jeffery came toward her. "I wouldn't if I were you. I'm not in the mood to have my kitchen all messed up. I have a guest coming."

"Well, fuck me, then let me hire you a maid service to come in." He drew back his hand just as the sounds of the crunch of gravel came through the doorway. Jeffery turned just as Blair stood up. Neither of them moved as Emerald came in the doorway.

The quietness was profound, and Emerald stood very still. Annabelle was afraid to say anything to Emerald for fear of scaring her. When she looked at Blair, then at Jeffery, she smiled.

"I got a ride home. I have to say this isn't what I expected to find in my kitchen when I got here." She glanced at Blair, then back at Jeffery. "You really don't think you're going to walk out of here, do you? You simply can't be that stupid."

"Shut the fuck up, cunt. I didn't come here for you, either." Blair growled at him, and Jeffery stopped moving toward Emerald. "You think this is funny, bitch? You think me being here is funny somehow?"

"I do, actually. And more so because you just don't get it. You're a dead man, and not only do you not see it, you think somehow you're going to come out on top." She laughed, put her backpack down on the floor, and moved slowly behind Blair. "I hope he lets you suffer for a little while before he rips your throat out."

"My throat? He's not going to get the chance to do anything more than sit there and let me do as I want. I've got something he wants." Annabelle felt a hand touch her arm and looked up at Sapphire as Jeffery babbled on. She helped her stand, and then she led her out of the room. She could still hear Jeffery as she sat down on the couch.

"I thought he was going to kill me." She put her head down between her knees and took slow, even breaths. "I know that Emerald will be fine in there with them, but could you please tell her to get out of there? I don't want to see her hurt, either."

Sapphire stood up and walked to the door again. Annabelle tried to calm her pounding heart, but she'd never been so afraid in all her days. When the timer went off in her pocket, she let out a scream that had Sapphire come running back, and she shoved the timer at her.

"It's for my pies. Damn him. If I burn them, I'm going to kill his butt. You know how much I hate wasting food." She looked up at Sapphire when she laughed. "I'm fine, dear, I really am. He scared me, that's all."

The first cruiser pulled in the drive, and she thought of Blair. Before she could say anything, she saw him come through the door and toward his room, his big wolf running like his tail was on fire. Annabelle giggled, something she'd not done in years, when she thought of the move that was going to happen soon. Blair moving to the smaller bedroom had been funny; him moving his stuff up four flights of stairs was going to be hilarious. The man had a lot of big furniture. Maybe they'd just share what Sapphire had. Annabelle had a feeling that the two of them would be partners in everything else, including furniture.

~~~

Sapphire put the last plate on the table when Blair walked in. He had pulled on a pair of gym shorts and a really beat up tee-shirt. She flushed when she had a sudden thought of his wolf and how he'd licked her until she came.

"He loved it." She looked up at him when he spoke. "You were thinking about my wolf and him tasting you. He loved it and your taste."

"I don't know what came over me to let him do that." She picked up the plate she'd just put down to set the table and held it in front of her. "Is that normal?"

"I've never done it before. Did it really bother you?" She shook her head no. "Good. Because I'm pretty sure he's going to do it again. I know I would. I love the taste of you in my mouth."

"Someone will hear you." She stepped back when he took the plate from her. "Blair, my family is just in the other room."

"I know. And unless they want to see me kiss you, I hope they stay there." He pulled her into his arms. "I need to talk to you anyway."

He held her for several minutes, and she realized that she really could get used to this. Having big, strong arms around her didn't just feel good. It made her feel good too. Silly, she thought, but that's how she felt. When he lifted her head up, she moaned, and he touched his lips to hers.

"You have any idea how much I'd like to lay you across the table and eat you?" She had a feeling she did know and ran her hand down over the front of his shorts. "Reach into my pants and take me into your hand."

She did as he asked and moaned when she realized he had no undershorts on. When she wrapped her hand around him, he rocked into her palm and turned her toward the wall. No one coming from the kitchen would be able to see what she was doing.

She felt the wall touch her back, and he took her mouth. Christ, she was never going to get enough of this man. When his fingers grazed over her breast, her nipple puckered and she moaned. He lifted his head, and she could see his need.

"Lift your blouse. I need to suckle at your nipple." She moved back, but before she could do as he asked, he pulled her blouse up along with her bra. His mouth was hot, and when he licked his tongue over her, then blew softly, she moaned again and tightened around his cock. When he suckled at her, she knew that she was going to come if he didn't stop now.

"Blair, someone is going to hear me when I come." She felt his growl across her breast. "Please, you have to know how close I am."

He lifted his head and picked her up. She had no idea where they were headed, but so long as he finished her off she didn't care. When she saw he was headed to his bedroom, she turned the doorknob as soon as they were near enough for her to do so. She was barely in the room before he was down on his knees before her.

"I want you to come like this." He pulled her shorts down and nipped at her through her panties. "Come hard so I can drink my fill of you."

His tongue entered her almost immediately after he moved her panties out of his way. She looked at the bed and sobbed when she pulled away from his incredible mouth.

"Bed. Please, before I fall." He nodded, and she backed to it only to have him push her back on it the moment her legs touched it. His mouth was over her; his tongue seemed to be everywhere. When he lifted her legs up and put them over his shoulders, she cried out when he suckled hard on her clit. When his fingers entered her, she rode them as quickly as he fucked her. As soon as he bit her clit again, she climaxed so hard she felt her vision blur. Then he stood up.

Sitting up on the edge of the bed, she reached for him. His cock was so hard and straining against the silky fabric that she fondled him through them. When he pulled them down just far enough for him to be free, she took him into her mouth and cupped his balls.

"I want to come this way. Fucking that pretty mouth of yours until I shoot my load down your throat." She moaned, and he growled. "I can feel that. Feel your throat make those noises as it runs through you and over my cock."

Sucking him this way was much easier than on her knees. He had control over his thrusts, and she could touch a great deal more of him than before. Cupping his balls in her hand, she felt how heavy and hot they were. He put his hands on either side of her face, and she moaned when he touched the back of her throat. He made her gag. She started to pull away, swallowing hard. She felt him stiffen as he slid down the back of her throat. She swallowed again.

"Christ," he shouted as he stiffened. The first taste of his cum nearly had her gagging again, but he held her still as he fucked her harder and harder. Her entire body felt him, and she reached between her legs and touched her clit.

She was swollen and hard and nearly bucked up off the bed when she brushed her fingers over her. When she did it again, Sapphire felt herself coming closer to the edge until she was ready to fall. Blair took a step back from her, his cock glistening wet with her saliva.

"Let me fuck you." She lay back, never taking her fingers from her pussy. He picked her up so quickly she nearly cried out and may have had his mouth not covered hers in a hot deep kiss. As soon as she was touching the wall, her back against it, she felt his cock at her entrance, and he brought her down hard.

In seconds she was screaming out another release. He continued to fuck her over and over against the wall even as she felt another climax racing over her. When she threw back her head to scream, he cried out too, his cock so deep inside of her she felt as if he touched her womb. He came gripping her ass to him even as she felt her body grow weak from exhaustion. Sleep claimed her before she knew if he came or not.

When she woke, the room was dark. She reached for him, knowing that she wasn't in her room but his, and found that she was alone. Sitting up, she reached for the lamp that she knew was there and turned it on. The room flooded in painful light.

Sapphire sat up and realized how sore she was. Her body ached in places she hadn't realized she'd used. When she stood up and moved to the bathroom, she noticed that it wasn't nearly as late as she'd thought and looked at her cell phone that had been laid over some of her clothes on the bathroom counter. It was only five o'clock. Turning on the shower, she decided that she'd try to work out some of the kinks with some warm water.

When she came out of the bathroom, she was already dressed. Diamond was sitting in one of the chairs that Blair had brought with him when he'd moved in. Was that only a week ago? Diamond didn't look happy. Sapphire sat on the bed and waited, knowing that Diamond would get to it sooner or later.

"Jeffery is being taken before the Board. They are going to either put him in their version of jail or have him put down." Sapphire nodded, knowing that her sister wasn't upset by either prospect. "He hurt me."

"I know he did, baby, and I'm so sorry that I couldn't keep that from happening." Sapphire knew that he'd hurt her more than the others, but she would never tell her what happened that night. She hoped she would now.

"You couldn't have done anything if you had been here, and if you had, we might have all died. He would have ended your life because he knew that you'd kill him if he did anything to us." She stood and walked to the room's only window. "He was going to rape us, him, and all his men. Harris was...he tried to save us, but he had him chained up too."

"Did he rape you?" Sapphire hadn't known about Harris being chained. She'd assumed all this time he'd been helping his brother. Not willingly, but helping all the same. "Diamond, did Jeffery hurt you that night? More than I saw when you took me away? What did he do if he didn't rape you?"

"He marked me. Not with his mouth but with his semen. He stood over me and...and came over me. I know that the other men can smell him on me. And none of them will come to me because of it. My mate could be out there and he'll not come near me because I've been marked by a bastard." She heard her sister sob as she continued. "I want to ask Blair if he can smell him, but I'm so ashamed that I let this happen."

"You didn't let anything happen. He took. And had you tried to fight him back he would have killed you. We both know that. I don't even know how I survived attacking him." Sapphire got up, walked behind her sister, and wrapped her arms around her. "I can ask Blair if you want. He has his scent now, so he'll be able to tell."

"I'm afraid of his answer." Sapphire understood that. "What if he's there? What if I can't ever find a mate because of him?"

"You will, and he'll be fucking lucky you've consented to be with him. And if he doesn't, I'll kick his ass. You know I can, too." Diamond laughed just as Sapphire wanted her to. "I love you, Diamond. And I always will."

"I know you will. And I love you, too. I'm so glad you and Blair worked things out between you. I've never seen you look so happy." She turned in her arms and smiled. "Grandmother said to come and tell you supper is on the table. I got sidetracked when I saw that we were alone."

"She said she invited Allen. Do you think he'll flirt with Grandmother again?" Both women giggled as she opened the door. "I think he's so cute the way he tries so hard."

Blair was standing there when she stepped out of the room, and she felt her body respond to how close he was. When his nostrils flared, she looked at her sister. Diamond nodded to him and moved away.

Chapter 14

"We have to talk. As soon as dinner is over, I need—"
She shook her head, and he took a deep breath. He'd hoped
that he had things in his mind set better, but she wasn't
going to wait.

"Tell me now. If it's bad news, I want it now and not
later. What's happened? Did Jeffery get away and he's out
there again?" He shook his head. "Then he's killed again.
Who? So help me, if he's touched one hair on my sister's
head, I'm going to—"

"It's not about him, not directly anyway. And remind
me to never piss you off. You're scary." He kissed her on
the mouth softly and took her hand. "We have a new pack."

He waited for her to say something and wasn't
disappointed when she finally did. "I didn't know *we* had an
old one other than us. Where did we acquire another one?"

"It's what's left of Jeffery's. And as my mate and
you're an alpha, they're your pack, too. We now have over
a hundred with Jeffery's." She shook her head, and he
frowned. "You don't want them? Okay, but they would
have to leave the area then. I can't have them just being
here without a governing body to watch over them."

"No, I mean I'm not an alpha." She glared at him when he snorted at her. "Well, I'm not. I'm just a normal wolf, a pack member. If you expect me to help you run a pack, you're going to be very disappointed in me."

"I highly doubt I could ever be disappointed in anything you do." He looked back toward the kitchen, then at her and smiled. "If I prove to you you're an alpha, too, will you reconsider helping me? I have to have your help. I don't have a clue how to do this on my own."

"How do you propose to show me that I'm an alpha? Make me order someone around?" This time she snorted. "I'm very good at ordering people around, in the event you didn't notice."

"I've noticed." He felt her stiffen and wondered if she had taken his complement as an insult. He'd meant it as a good thing, but the look on her face made him think she'd not taken it that way. He pulled her along to the dining room and then through to the kitchen where he knew they all were.

"Ask him." She frowned at him, obviously not understanding what he meant. "Ask Harris or even my dad what you are. Go on, ask them."

"What's going on?" Harris took a step toward her and Blair growled low. The man stopped immediately. Blair had no idea where the thought of killing the man had come from, but he was glad he'd stopped when he had.

"She thinks she's not an alpha." Blair looked at the two men standing there, then at her grandmother when she laughed. He smiled, too, as he continued. "I don't know how to convince her other than letting her do something alpha-like."

"Not an alpha? My goodness child, you're more of an alpha than my mate was." His dad looked at her, then at him as he smiled at Sapphire. "His mother was good, honey, but you're top of the line. Christ, it's like you were born to the job. Which I guess now is correct."

"She was." They all looked at Annabelle. "Her mother was the same way. She would never let anyone feel her power over them, but everyone knew it all the same. My son did, as well. He was fiercely proud of her. All of the girls are prone to be alphas, but you're right, Sapphire is very strong."

"Why?" Sapphire flushed and looked around the room before she continued. "Why am I an alpha? I mean, what makes you see it when others don't?"

"Jeffery did." Harris looked at him for permission to speak, and Blair gave it to him with a short nod. "Jeffery knew what you were long before he took the pack. He told me that was the reason he had to have it, because he had to destroy you. But then he realized that you had no idea you were stronger than him, and he relished in the fact that he could control you when all along you were the apparent leader over him."

"There's no such thing as a female alpha." She looked at him, and he shook his head at her at her fearful statement. "I can't be an alpha."

He laughed; he couldn't help it. "You're this big, bad-assed female, but mention the fact that you're an alpha and you fall apart? Nah, you're too strong for that. And you are an alpha female. And I love you for it."

"You're not going to convince her with that logic, I'm afraid." Diamond stepped forward as she looked at her sister. "She's going to have to have some proof. It used to irritate me as a kid how she never just believed anything without some sort of tangible thing. *Tell Harris to shift.*"

Blair looked at Sapphire to see if she'd heard her sister's last statement, too. She'd whispered it through his mind and knew that she'd done it so that they could both hear. When Sapphire looked up at him, he knew she had.

Just say to him 'shift.' He'll either do it because he has no choice or he'll just stare at you with a dumbfounded look on his face. He watched her closely, waiting for her to respond. *Sapphire, I swear to you that this will work, and you'll see that you're what I need for you to be, what we all need for you to be.*

She nodded, and he wanted to tell her to forget it. She looked so afraid, a look he'd never seen on her face before. When he wrapped his arms around her, she relaxed a little, and he kissed her neck. She looked at Harris and smiled at him, and he smiled back. Then she uttered a single word at him.

His body responded immediately. There was no simple shift of human to wolf, but an immediate and profound slap-him-in–the-face shift to wolf. In seconds gone was the enforcer, and in his place a whimpering wolf. He shied away from her when Sapphire went to him.

"I didn't think it would hurt him." She reached her hand out slowly as she snarled at him. "You fucking bastard, he's hurting."

"He's not hurt. I swear to you he's just startled, that's all." Blair reached for the counter and held on as he continued. "To tell you the truth, I'm a little freaked out myself. I thought...shit, I don't know, I thought he'd just shift like we do."

Harris went to her, rubbed his muzzle along her hand, and then sat near her. Blair was afraid Harris wouldn't let him go near his mate, but when he knelt down, Harris did the same to him, marking them both. When his dad slowly approached, Harris bared his canines but didn't move from them.

"He's yours now, Sapphire. You've called his wolf, and now he will protect you with his life." She turned to look at his dad as he told her what would happen now. "When you call an enforcer's wolf, he attaches himself to you as your protector. He'll keep an eye on Blair as well, but he'll protect you over him. He belongs to you as much as Blair does."

"I don't understand this. Why didn't anyone ever tell me this?" She looked at him, then at her grandmother. "Did you know all this?"

"No. Your mother didn't participate in a pack, and your father did only when it was necessary because of your mom's abilities. They thought to hide them from everyone. Had they have taken a pack or even joined one over the years, I might have learned more, but...." She shrugged. "I only know what I've read. Until Jeffery took the pack in our little town, I'd never had anyone approach us to be members before. He made it impossible to remain on the outside looking in."

Blair was worried for Sapphire. She looked simply lost. He wanted to pull her into his arms, but there was something so...he supposed so hard looking about her. When he glanced at Harris, he moved toward his new mistress and put his muzzle on her thigh. For whatever reason, he no longer felt the surge of jealously toward the man and didn't want to murder him. He looked at his dad when he felt him touch his mind.

Your wolf knows what he is to her and accepts him. Blair looked back at the two of them as he continued. *He'll not leave her. Ever. He'll kill for her and be killed for her now. It doesn't happen often that an enforcer is pulled by anyone but the male alpha, but she's very strong.*

Stronger than me? The words slipped out before he could stop them. His dad smiled and shook his head. He wasn't relieved like he thought he'd be. He felt the need to protect her even more.

She's your equal. And the two of you will run a powerful pack because of it. She'll make decisions as if she had you standing next to her agreeing, and you'll do the same. You're one person. When either of you are confronted, you'll be able to solve it head-on and as one. His dad laughed. *Son, I'm going to take great pleasure in pledging my wolf to this pack. And so you know, I'm looking forward to you having a pack of pups all on your own. Christ, I hope they're all just like her.*

Blair looked at Sapphire when she stood up and turned to him. He smiled. She'd come to a decision and it was going to be monumental. Then she smiled. Christ, he had no idea who was going to be at the receiving end of whatever was going through her mind, but he was glad it wasn't him.

"I want to go see Jeffery. I have a few things I need to discuss with him." Blair nodded at her. "And when we return we're going to call a meeting, if you don't mind. We also have something to say to this new pack we inherited."

"All right." He smiled back at her. "But I'd like to talk to Diamond first." Blair had heard from Sapphire about what had happened, and he wanted to speak to her about it. She was worried, he could tell, but now was having as good a time as ever. He took her to the office and had her sit while Sapphire sat near her. This wasn't going to be easy.

~~~

The meeting had gone well, Sapphire thought. Diamond had believed Blair when he told her he smelled that no wolf had marked her in any way. She did smell of wolf, him and his dad mostly, but nothing more than a brush of skin against skin. And now she and Blair were on their way to the Board to have a conversation with Jeffery, and Diamond was as happy as she'd ever been before that fateful night.

"I've never been in the cells before. Have you?" Blair shook his head. "You think they'll keep him away from us? Or I guess me from him?"

"If there are any humans there, they won't know what you are until you tell them." Blair looked over at her for a second, then back at the road before he spoke again. "Are you going to tell them?"

"I'm not telling anyone anything. I'm going to prove a point, but I'm not going to do anything more than that." She smiled at his groan. "Jeffery will get what he deserves. Not all of it, but some. I'm going to make him understand that fucking with my family is no longer an option. I don't know why, but I have a feeling he might try something from his cell to harm them if he can."

Blair nodded. She waited for him to tell her to let him handle this, or even worse, for her to not do anything stupid. She would have hurt him badly for either comment, but all he did was look out the front window. They were pulling into the parking lot when he reached for her hand and looked at her.

"I want to keep you from being hurt. I know that you can handle whatever happens, but you have to know that even though you're my equal, I still want you safe." She nodded. "A large part of me wants to drive back to the house and take you into the woods and make love to you near the waterfall, but you need this more than I do. Besides we have the rest of our lives to be together, and I understand that this is something you have to do."

"I have to make him see that he's not beaten me. I don't know if he thinks that or not, but I want him to see that for all his harm to me and mine, I'm still going strong and happier than I've ever been in all my life." He pulled her to him and kissed her hard. Then he got out of the truck, came around to her side, and opened her door.

"My lady." She laughed at him when he bowed. Helping her out, she was startled when he pressed her against the side of his truck and rocked his cock into her. She moaned when he cupped her ass and brought her up against him.

"Blair, people are going to see us." He nipped at her throat, and she felt the small wound bleed a little. "You keep that up and I'm going to come right now."

"Good. You should go in there smelling of sex and me." He rocked again. "I want you to come for me. Let me make you come so that I can taste you."

Her body flared to life just like it did every time she thought of him and sex. Not that whenever he touched her, came near her, or even walked in the same town as her, she didn't want him. But right now, knowing that they were being watched and where she was going made her spread her legs a little and cup his cock in her palm.

He devoured her mouth, and his tongue danced along hers, quick and hard. She was going to come just from his kisses if he kept this up. When he lifted her up so that her groin was flush with his, she wrapped her legs around him and rode him.

"Come for me." He rocked into her over and over, and she moaned as he slid his mouth down her throat to her shoulder. "I wish I could be sucking your pussy right now. I know you'd be flooding me with juices." She closed her eyes, thinking about what he was saying to her and how much she wanted him to do just what he said.

The first image appeared in her mind, and she looked at him. When they started to flow past her vision quicker and quicker, she knew it was him. He was sending her memories of their time together. The one where he was mounting her from behind as a wolf, then the one where his wolf had licked her until she came made her grip him tighter to her.

"You liked that didn't you?" She nodded, unable to form a word. "My wolf did as well. He knew what you were before we did, and he wanted his mate. Would you let him do that again? Lick you until you come hard again?"

"Yes." Sapphire closed her eyes tighter and brought up her own memory of what he'd done to her, and felt Blair's need double. "We should find a place to fuck. I need you inside of me now."

"We can't, not yet anyway. Fuck, I want you." He reached behind her and held her as he fucked her against the truck. She felt it move behind her and wondered if he'd tip it over as hard as he was thrusting into her. "Come. Come now before I fucking explode."

Throwing back her head, she let out a primal howl that curled her toes as her body did just what he commanded her to do. She knew Blair was going to bite her and tilted back her head to give him whatever he needed as another powerful climax tore through her. When he sank his teeth into her, she screamed out his name. Sapphire held onto Blair as tightly as she could when he tore at her flesh and scarred her.

He continued to rock in her as her body shuddered through several smaller but powerful climaxes. She looked up at him when he lifted his head from her throat. She nearly came again when she saw the blood on his lip and licked it from him.

"You're going to hurt when we get home. I'm not going to be gentle, and when I run you down, your wolf is going to hurt as well. There is no fucking way I'm going to be able to be gentle with you." She smiled at him as he helped her stand up. "I'm in pain, love."

She cupped his cock again, and he grabbed her wrist. "I could take you into my mouth and help you."

"You take me into your mouth and we're going to get arrested. And I'd just as soon not have to explain why my wife and I were arrested for indecent exposure." She didn't hear anything he said past wife and seemed to know it. "I have something for you. I wanted to wait until later, but I want you to have it now."

He reached into his pocket and handed her a little blue box. She didn't take it right away but kept her hands fisted until he opened her left one and put it there. Sapphire was afraid to open it.

"Whether you open it now or later you're going to have to give me an answer." She nodded at him, and he laughed. "I'm sure that it's not going to be often that I render you speechless, but it does have its merits."

He took the box from her and opened it. He'd done it in a way that she'd not seen the contents. But when he dropped to his knees before her she wanted to tell him to get up before someone saw them. Stupid, considering that she had no such qualms just moments ago when she was screaming out his name in the best climax she'd ever had.

The ring slipped onto her finger just to the second knuckle. She could see a wide band but nothing more. When she looked at him, she felt herself fall deeper in love with Blair and wondered if she'd ever not want to toss him to the floor and have her way with him.

"You keep looking at me like that and all my good intentions are going to go out the window." He cleared his throat as he continued. "Sapphire Erickson, will you please do me the upmost honor in becoming my partner in life? My mate in all things and my equal in our pack? Will you marry me and become my wife and partner in that way, as well?"

"I don't know what I'm doing." He grinned and kissed her hand before sliding the ring all the way on. "I didn't say yes."

He kissed her when he stood up. "No, you didn't, but you didn't say no, either. Come on, let's get this over with so I can take you home and make love to you all night and into the morning."

They entered the big building that looked from the outside like a large hotel. But in reality it was a huge holding place for rogues that were either awaiting trial or had been sentenced and were there to serve whatever the courts had assigned them whether it was death or life in a silver-lined cell. Most of the time they were simply put to death, and Sapphire knew that when everything came out about Jeffery, he'd be on that list as well.

They were shown to a large room. She'd never been there before either and was nervous about the large silver loop that was in one corner of the room. There were no windows in this room, and it was devoid of all furniture. There were three cameras hanging high on the walls, all of them pointing at the hook in the corner. There was only the one door other than the one they'd entered from, and both were covered in silver. A human had let them in five minutes ago.

She and Blair said nothing but held hands waiting for whatever was to come. She could feel that he was nervous as well, and when the other door opened, both of them jumped slightly. She had a feeling that not only had the guards seen them, but Jeffery as well. She was sure of it when he spoke after being chained to the loop.

"So, the big, bad Sapphire is afraid of a little sound. Oh my, how the mighty have fallen." She didn't comment on the fact that he was the one chained up, not her, as he continued. "What the fuck do you think you're doing here? Come to testify on my behalf?"

"Not fucking likely since I'm part of the reason you're here." She smiled when he snarled at her. "Now, how does it feel, Jeffery, to know that you at one time had it all and now you're reduced to nothing more than a silver-lined room with chains on your ankles and wrists? You can't even shift if you want to."

"You'd be surprised at what I can still do, my dear. Just you wait and see. What the fuck do you want?" She leaned against the wall and stared at him. She had no idea what she'd come for to be honest.

Chapter 15

Sapphire had had this long list of things she'd wanted to ask Jeffery. Things she'd wanted to say to him as well. Blair knew because he'd seen her write them out on the way there. He'd hoped that she'd realize that he wouldn't give her anything but lies and more questions that she'd have no answers for. Sapphire stared at Jeffery until he looked at Blair.

"So? You've hooked yourself up with the Erickson family. You'll regret it. Fucking her won't get you what you want because I've made sure of that." Blair didn't say anything, nor did he change his expression. He'd learned to be good at bluffing when he'd been in college and playing poker with the richer kids. It had helped support him during his leaner years.

Jeffery seemed to grow angrier at him because he wasn't playing along. Blair didn't care. He could wait all day if need be. Blair hoped that if he turned to Sapphire, and he was sure he would, he'd get the same blank stare until the man completely lost it. This was going to be epic.

"Don't you want to know what I've taken from you?" Still nothing from Sapphire, so Jeffery looked at him again to try and get him to ask him what the hell he was talking about. "Surely you want to know. You want to know what I've so perfectly taken from you that you'll never get back."

The longer they stood there staring at him, the madder he got until he finally snapped. When Jeffery snarled at them to ask what it was, the guard that had been standing just behind them stepped forward with a long club in his hand. He'd raised it high in the air to no doubt put Jeffery back in line. Blair stopped him with a raised hand.

"Whatever it is you think you've taken, I surely hope you enjoy it. For the next few days at least. Because, from what we were told, that's about all you have left in this world before they take you out back and shoot you with a silver bullet." Jeffery lunged at Blair, but he wasn't finished yet. "We've taken your pack, your brother has now become enforcer to Sapphire, and once you have been declared dead to us, and I might point out to you that has already happened as far as we're concerned, we'll gain all you left behind."

"You lie." Jeffery looked at her, he supposed for conformation. But she didn't say anything to him. But when he lunged at her, she moved just within his reach and stood there.

Blair wasn't sure what she had in mind but didn't let the guard interfere. The smile on his face was a little odd, but Blair held him back. She needed this; whatever it was, she needed this to settle things between the two of them. When he backed off from her stare, Blair let go of his pent up breath. He knew she could handle herself, but that didn't make him any less afraid for her.

"Do you know what I hate most about you?" He backed up another step, and she took one forward so that she was now within the length of his chain. "I hate a great deal about you, but there is one thing that I can't stand about you."

She waited, and Blair had to bite his inner lip so he wouldn't laugh. She was turning the tables on Jeffery by making him ask her for answers. Jeffery moved back from her as far as possible. The guard stepped forward as if to take charge, and Blair moved in front of him and let a little of his wolf go. The man backed off.

"What are you talking about?" He glanced back at Sapphire and Jeffery just as the guard moved back. And if he hadn't, he might have missed what happened next. He knew for as long as he lived he would never forget it.

Jeffery lunged at her, and since she was close enough for him to touch, he raked his hand down her face. The shift from human to wolf was instantaneous; one second Sapphire was standing there, and the next she was a snarling fucking pissed off wolf. She stood on her hind legs and hit Jeffery with her entire body.

He tore the chains from his hands, and Blair had a second, no more than that, to think that he shouldn't have been able to do that when the ones around his legs came lose as well. Jeffrey shifted into his wolf, but he was no match for Sapphire. She had him pinned to the floor before his wolf was fully formed.

Sapphire went for his throat, and Jeffery couldn't get away quickly enough before she had his wolf down and her mouth over his exposed throat. The smallest move on his part would have her ripping it out. Blair looked at the man who was supposed to be guarding them and hit him square in the face. He fell to the floor in a heap. The fucking prick had helped him hurt his mate.

Blair moved to where Sapphire and Jeffery were and crouched down to speak to him. This wasn't going to end well for the idiot. Blair smiled; nope, not going to end well for either man, including the one that was bleeding on the floor with a uniform on.

"You paid him off somehow." Jeffery blinked at him. "You can speak to me. With my mate no doubt tasting your blood, we have a connection now. Did you pay off the guard?"

Yes. Get her the fuck off me or so help me I'll—

"You'll do nothing unless you want her to tear your throat out. She may yet, but for now she's going to get the answers she wants." Blair ran his hand down Sapphire's head and over her back. "Ask him, love, whatever it is, ask him so that we can both hear."

Why did you hurt my family? Why did you make our life so difficult while we were members of your pack? Blair waited with Sapphire, and when the door opened behind them and three guards walked in, he stood up and crossed his arms over his chest.

"You come in to do anything other than to pick up that piece of shit and you and I are going to have a go around. And just so you are all aware, I'm itching to kill someone." The front guard took a step back and bumped into the others as Blair continued. "I don't care if it's you or him, but somebody's going to pay for him almost getting my mate harmed."

"The operator, the one at the desk, has been...he'd dead. The president of the Board came in just as the she-alpha was jumped, and...and the president snapped his neck like it was nothing but a twig. The president said to tell you he's got your back, sir, and we were to...we were to do whatever you said." He swallowed hard and looked at Sapphire. "He said for us to do what you wanted or he'd let her deal with us. You won't do that, will you? We'll do everything...she took him down without your help at all."

"She did, didn't she? I'm quite proud of her actually." He kicked the first guard that was just beginning to stir. "I want to press charges against him. Benetton here just admitted that he'd paid this one off. I'm assuming he did the same to the operator as well."

It took the three of them to drag the man out, and when the guard woke again, just as they were clearing the hall, Blair heard the president of the Board speaking to him in low tones. He was telling him what was going to happen to him for harming an alpha of good standing, as well as what he was going to have to expect for aiding a criminal. Blair only half listened because he wanted to be with Sapphire.

He moved back to where she was and heard the tail end of something spewing from Benetton's mind. The man must want her to kill him was all he could think. He crouched down and touched her again, needing the contact with her more than ever. Blair could not wait for this shit to be finished.

"If you don't learn to control yourself, I'm going to do to you what the president has done to your accomplice. I would really enjoy snapping your neck like a twig, just so we're clear on that." Blair looked at Sapphire and could see her hurt, and wondered what the fuck the man had said to her. "Benetton, I'm going to take great pleasure in killing you."

She said she's some sort of alpha and that she's always been stronger than me. I think she's full of— Benetton screamed, and Blair let go of the laughter he'd been holding. *She's fucking going to kill me.*

"I would think that's a fair assumption. It's well within her rights as alpha to kill you for attacking her. And don't

KATHI S. BARTON

even tell me that you had no idea what she was. Harris already told us that you knew she was alpha, and your sole purpose was to destroy her. I think that you'll welcome the bullet over what she can do."

Admit it, you fucking bastard. Blair heard Benetton scream again when Sapphire screamed at him. *Admit you tried to kill me all those years ago, and I'll let you go.*

All right. Christ, all right, I tried to have you murdered. I tried everything in my power to have you fucking ended, but no matter what I tried, you'd land on your feet. Then I thought if I killed off the others you'd be so devastated that you'd simply crawl into a hole and I'd be able to finish you off once and for all. But you had to come back, you had to just do the opposite of what I'd had set up for you. This is entirely your fault. She let him go, and when he didn't move, Sapphire moved back well beyond the boundaries of the chain. Not that it mattered; he'd long since gotten free of it even if he'd ever been chained in the first place. She sat there as Blair moved back toward her, but before he could move, he was being knocked aside and his head hit the wall hard. Then nothing at all.

~~~

Harris watched the alpha and his mate as they paced the big office. He could hear them speaking, but not what was being said. He was too nervous to try to concentrate anyway. He knew he'd only hear something he didn't want to, so he thought of anything and everything other than what was going on in the office.

He'd been here for nearly four days, and no one had said anything about his brother. Not that Harris cared at that point, but with all the other things coming out into the open, he was afraid that Sapphire wouldn't want him to be there any longer, and he'd be without a pack. Not to mention the

180

thought of not protecting the big alphas made him sort of sick to his stomach. He had to protect them.

For as much as Harris hated his brother, he loved him as well. He was his only living relative, and though they'd never seen eye to eye on a great many things, especially things concerning the Erickson family, he was still blood. When Harris had been asked to come to the pack house, he'd packed up what little belongings he'd had and had them sitting in his car. He thought about what he'd heard three days ago and his conversation with Blair.

"You'll need to go and get whatever you have at the house. As of yesterday the Board has taken possession of it as well as the contents. There will be a guard at the house that will go with you to take what belongs only to you." Harris nodded and sat down. "There are things going on that I cannot discuss with you, but I promise you that when I can tell you, I will find you and let you know."

Harris nodded but didn't ask what he really wanted to know. "I didn't live at the big house with my brother. I did have a smallish place. If I could go there and get some of those things, I'd very much appreciate that. There isn't much, but it's mine." Blair nodded.

"I'll have one of the others take you over. I'm not sure if you had any monies coming to you either. Can you remember when you were last paid and what you were paid?" Harris had shaken his head before Blair had finished speaking. "You don't remember?"

"I was never paid. Jeffery said that he was giving me food and a roof over my head. That was good enough for me." Harris asked before he could think, "Do enforcers get paid for keeping someone safe?"

"Yes. You're putting your ass on the line daily. It's the least someone can do for you." Harris didn't know what to say so said nothing. "Harris, did Jeffery have any accounts that you knew about? Money in some bank that paid his pack members for working in his home?"

"He didn't pay anyone as far as I knew. If he did, it wasn't much. I thought…I guess we all thought we were lucky to have a pack at all, much less get paid for it. At least that's what he always told us." Harris had waited for more, but Blair had told him he'd contact him in a few days. And this morning a message had been sent for him to be here.

At ten before ten, Sapphire came out and asked him to join them. "We have a few things to tell you, and some things…well, come in and we'll get this squared away as quickly as we can."

Harris was overwhelmed, and he was pretty sure they knew it. And unlike his brother, they didn't make him feel like his feelings weren't justified or valid. He sat in the chair that Sapphire had pointed to and looked across the big desk at Blair. She handed him a bottle of water, which he took with a shaky hand.

"He's dead, isn't he?" Blair nodded, and Harris felt the weight of the world lifted from his shoulders. "I'll leave if you wish. I was actually afraid to do so before now. But with Jeffery dead, I won't have to be looking over my shoulder every ten minutes to make sure he's not there with a knife to ram in my back."

Harris stood up and moved back. He stopped when Blair said something, and he turned to ask him what he'd said.

"I said, are you leaving the pack for any other reason other than your brother being dead? Is it because Sapphire killed him? I assure you it was him or me, and I'm glad she stepped in. But there was no choice in the matter." Harris looked at Sapphire, then at Blair as he continued. "Of course, you're welcome to leave. I'd never think of making you stay where you didn't want. But we'd very much like you to be a member of our pack."

Harris sat down before he fell. He didn't know which was harder to believe, that Sapphire had killed his brother or that they wanted him to stay. He tried to think around his pounding heart. He had a pack and one that he was proud to call his own.

"Harris, are you all right?" He nodded at Blair. "Do you want to leave us? If you do, is there anything we can do to convince you to stay?"

"No. Yes. I mean no." He took a deep breath, and when that felt good, he took another. "I don't want to leave. Yes, I want to stay, and no, there is nothing you need to do to have me stay."

They smiled at him, and Sapphire finally sat down. He'd known, he supposed, that she was nervous, but not why. She leaned back and looked at Blair before she looked back at him.

"Jeffery attacked Blair when his back was turned. He had already tried to hurt me, but I'd…I guess I got the better of him before he could do much more than scrape my cheek. I'm very sorry, but he might have killed Blair had I not intervened. I ended up tearing his throat out. The Board just last night told me they were ruling it justified." Harris nodded at her, and she looked away, and he knew she'd been more than just physically hurt, but he'd hurt her heart, too. "He said that he'd thought to kill off my family to bring me to my knees. Then he was planning to kill me. Did you know that?"

"Not until afterwards. It was right after you left that I started making plans to leave. But that night I was getting ready to move out when I was jumped. They chained me to a tree, and I had to watch it all. I was let go after it was all over and went to see to your grandmother immediately. I couldn't find you at all. Then I was told that Diamond had hidden you away." He moved around on the chair, feeling better with every word that passed over his lips. "It was within my rights to leave when he clawed me open and left me for dead. I disavowed myself of him and his pack immediately." He looked at Blair. "What happens to the rest of the pack? There aren't that many left, but what few there are will need guidance."

"The Board has asked me to take them. I'm not sure I'm ready for that, but they seemed to think we'll do just fine." Harris had to laugh. He supposed for a man as much a loner as Blair was, it would be difficult to take on not only a mate but a hundred other pack members as well.

"You'll help us, of course?" He nodded at Sapphire when she asked. "Good, we're glad to hear that, because we have a slight problem. Money was found when your brother was taken. A great deal of money, as a matter of fact. We need you to help us get it to the others in the pack so they can have a fresh start, too."

"Me?" He stood up, then sat back down. "I know we all need something more than we had, but I've no idea…Christ, they'll want things I don't know how to get them."

"We can get them what they'll need. Everyone that works for us from now will be paid a decent wage, as well as we're upgrading the houses and adding a facility here for health and well-being. Once we have that taken care of here, we'll sell the other house and grounds and move everyone here." Blair leaned back in his chair as he continued. "The house there is going to need some work. Most of it is going to be easy—carpet and paint. The grounds need to be maintained so that it looks good for the new buyer. Then once we have everything ready here, we'll keep some of the pack there to watch over it until it's sold. Sapphire and I have just purchased another seven hundred acres thanks to the Board helping us out."

"And you plan to pour that money back into the pack?" Blair nodded and smiled. "I don't think I like the look you're giving me right now. What haven't you told me?"

"Nothing much except that you'll have a car as well as an allowance to make sure things are maintained and in ship shape order. You'll have the authority to set and enforce all rules as well as have the full backing of Sapphire and I whenever you need it. And then there's the other stuff." Blair looked at Sapphire and winked. Then she took over.

"You'll be training some of the men how to do certain projects for us, namely being on an enforcer squad. And when I say men, I mean both sexes. We want you to make sure that when the time comes for a pack to do their best, they'll able to help with people like Jeffery." Harris nodded, and when Blair handed him a file, he opened it as Sapphire continued. "These are the other jobs we want to see if we can get some training on. We don't expect you to do all the work, but make sure that standards are met as well as people being rewarded for doing a good job."

By the time that Harris left, he had a better understanding of his new alphas and a great deal more respect. Plus, he now had his first paycheck and a car that ran all the time instead of when it suited it. He drove over to his brother's house just to see what was going on. He was surprised to see that work had already begun and that the place looked better already. Harris had never been so happy to have a job in his entire life.

As he drove back to the house he'd been staying in since he'd gotten out of the hospital, he thought about what his life might be like now. He was going to be the best enforcer he could be now, and no more shortcuts, either. Harris wanted to be the man he'd never been with his brother for the simple reason that the new alphas deserved the best. Harris was going to give it to them. Smiling for the first time in a great long while, Harris decided that life was suddenly sunshine and green grass wonderful.

Chapter 16

"Do you think he'll have any trouble?" Sapphire sat back in the chair after getting her and Blair a glass of iced tea. "I know that he doesn't think he'll be able to do it, but I know he can."

"He'll make it work, and much better than we thought. My biggest concern is whether or not to take you across this desk or to wait until I get you naked out in the woods." She felt her body respond to his words. "Of course, I could take you here *and* there if you're up to it."

"I'm sort of up to it." She smiled at him when he growled low. "You're sure you're up for a challenge like that? I mean just this morning you were complaining about not getting enough sleep."

"I was talking about the phone ringing fifty times in the middle of the night. Who was calling anyway that we had to hear it?" She had heard it too but was used to it now.

"Diamond is on call for the rest of the week, and they have to call her when there are problems with a patient. She said she'd make sure that they call on her cell from now on. She'd forgotten that you could hear it too." Sapphire stretched her body and watched Blair as his eyes darkened.

She wanted him as badly as he looked like he wanted her, but she wanted to tease him too.

"You do know that you're playing with fire, don't you?" She nodded at him and stood up. "Take off your clothes. I want to see you spread out over the desk before I feast on you."

"You have too much shit on this desk for me to lie there very comfortably." She burst out laughing when he stood up and swiped his hand over the top of the lovely oak and threw all the papers to the floor. "That's one way to do it, I suppose."

"Come here for me." She didn't move but began to unbutton her blouse slowly. "You should probably lock the door first. When you scream, I don't want the household coming in here to rescue you again."

Last night they'd been making love in the shower, and when she'd cried out her release, her sister Emerald had burst in the room with a gun. They had since found out that she had it registered and used it walking around campus at night. Blair had told her that he wanted her to have self-defense classes, and Sapphire agreed. Emerald and a gun just didn't seem all that safe. Sapphire walked over and turned the lock, and moved slowly back toward Blair.

"Do you have any idea how much I love the way you look when you start to get aroused? I love the way you smell, too, the way your skin seems to take on a glow that makes me want to lick every part of you." She had to lean into the chair that was just in front of her when he started to speak. She was glad now that she'd taken the time to lock the door. They were about to get very noisy in here.

"Take off your tie and shirt for me." He stood up to do as she asked. He did it like he did everything, with a slowness that set her on edge. But this time she enjoyed his taking his time.

When he was down to his tee shirt and pants, she moved closer to him. On most men, a sleeveless tee shirt seemed so trashy, but Blair wore his just a little too snug, and she loved the way his furred chest hairs tufted out from the top of them. He unbuckled his belt but let it hang onto his pants while he opened his fly.

"You've slowed down. Would you like for me to help you?" She nodded at his husky question. "I'm all for tearing your clothes from you rather than waiting for you to take them off. Besides, I love the sound of clothes being torn. It reminds me of you shifting while dressed and knowing that you're going to be naked when the time comes for you to be human again."

He moved toward her and finished unbuttoning her blouse. She had on a skirt because they'd had a meeting with Galloway Industries that morning and she'd wanted to look nice. Now all she could think about was Blair lifting the skirt up over her hips and taking her from behind. When he dropped to his knees in front of her, she had to grab onto his head to keep from falling.

"Blair, I thought you were going to lay me over your desk. You've gotten it all cleaned up for me." He grinned as he ran his hands up under her skirt and into the tiny strings on the hips of her panties. "You can untie them."

"And what fun would that be?" She moaned when he tore them off her. "The next time you wear a skirt, don't wear panties. I want to know that you're ready for me whenever we're together."

She nodded and would have agreed to anything right now. He inched her skirt up and kissed each thigh every time he exposed a little more of her. She was a living flame by the time he had it up far enough that her pussy was showing.

"You're wet for me." She nodded suddenly, so needy she was ready to beg him to do something, anything to relieve the ache he was causing. "I want to drink from you this way before I put you on my desk."

"Why?" Sapphire had to try three times before she could say the little word where it didn't sound like she was strangling it out. But he seemed to understand her.

"Because this way your juices run down your legs and I can lick it. When you're laid out for me, I miss some, and that simply won't do." She shook her head, not really caring if it would do or not. His fingers slid up over her pussy and down to her other thigh. She was trembling now.

"Blair, please, I'm not going to be able to stand like this for much longer." He smiled at her as his finger slid in and out of her. She wanted to beg him to finish her, but she'd learned over the past few days that the more she begged him the longer he seemed to make her suffer. When he finally reached in and licked her clit, she nearly came up off the floor.

"You're ready right now, aren't you?" She nodded at him. "Would you like to come? If I let you, will you let me take you from behind while I smack your pretty ass?"

"Please, Blair, I don't care what you do, just help me come." She nearly screamed when he sucked her clit into his mouth, and did scream when he nipped at her. Her climax was fast and hard, but not nearly as satisfying as she needed. But he picked her up and sat her in front of the desk. When she gripped the edge, he moved her more over the top.

"Hang onto the other side. You're going to need the leverage for what I have in mind." She did as he asked, her body already ready for him to do his worst. The sting across her rear cheek had her moaning, and when he smacked her twice more, she rolled her hips, looking for something to fill her.

"Fuck me, Blair, please. I need to feel your cock in me while you beat my ass." He chuckled at her, and she heard him moving his clothes. As soon as his cock touched her ass, she stiffened.

"No, I'm not going to fuck you here. Not yet at any rate. I just want to play." His hand came down twice more, and she relaxed again. "That's my girl. I'm going to fuck you like this someday, but for now, I just want to ready this pretty hole for me."

His fingers ran through her curls, not once touching her where she needed it most. When he pressed against her ass, she tried to relax, but she was afraid of the pain she was sure that was going to be there.

"Relax, baby, I swear to you you'll enjoy this." As he moved his soaking fingers over her tight bud, he reached to her pussy and began moving in and out of her. "You're so wet right now I could fuck you, and you'd be able to take all of me."

"Please." She rolled back against his body to be rewarded with another slap. But she was almost too far gone to quit now. If he smacked her enough she'd come or he'd fuck her and she'd come. Either way, she was going to get what she needed most. When he pressed deep into her ass, she nearly came up off the table, but he held her down.

"I'm going to fuck you now. I almost can't wait to do this." He put his free hand on her hip and held her while he moved into her slowly. She tried to force him to go deeper, but he wasn't having it. He was fully in her, and she stilled when he commanded her to.

~~~

Blair felt the sweat roll down his back as he tried to remain as still as he could. If she moved or he did, he was coming, and there would be no stopping him. When she moaned, he actually thought about coming, then giving her whatever she wanted after. His balls were so tight against his body he wanted to cup them. He leaned over her and bit her ear lobe.

"I want you to be very still. If you move, I'm going to come, and then you'll be left high and dry." She moaned, and he felt her stiffen. It wasn't going to work. Breathing made him want to shoot his load deep inside of her.

"I'm so wet and so very close right now. If you touched me, I'd come with you." He shivered at her words and the tone. She sounded like sex. Hot silky sex, and she was all his. He reached between her legs and touched her swollen clit.

Moving slowly inside of her, he pinched her. She hadn't been kidding when she said she was wet and close. His fingers slid over her quickly, and when he stroked her again, she came apart with a scream, bringing him along with her. Standing up behind her, he grabbed her hips and took her as hard as he could. Blair threw back his head and howled. His wolf even seemed to enjoy himself.

Falling back in his chair, he brought her with him. She lay across him so limply he had to smile. He loved rendering her to the point where he could hold her quietly like this. When she finally stirred enough to turn in his lap, he cradled her in his arms and kissed her head. Blair didn't think he'd ever been so content before meeting her.

"I have a meeting with Thad tomorrow. He wants to go over the specs again at his plant. They're having problems with seals around the veggies. I think he's got a problem with his foreman down there. Morton Guzman is a prince." Blair laughed. He hadn't cared for the man much either.

"I've been thinking about our newest client. Do you think he'll ever figure out that his secretary is a panther and we're wolves? The poor man seems to be completely focused on his work. Poor guy, how will he ever smell the roses doing that all the time?" She slapped his arm. "I'll have you know I smelled a few roses in my time. How do you think I convinced you to be my mate?"

She snorted. "Yeah, right. You did a bang-up job convincing me, all right." She stood up and reached for her shirt. "Should we tell him you think? I don't mean right away but eventually?"

He'd thought of it, too. He really liked the man and enjoyed working with him. It was nice to have a person believe in you so soundly that he would simply do it without question. There was no doubt this was going to be a money maker for him, and the new contract he and Sapphire had signed guaranteed that they would be making a great deal, too.

He pulled his pants up over his hips without standing. He reached for his phone when it rang and grinned at Sapphire when she sat across from him. His dad was missing him, and he and Sapphire had decided to have him move into the big house, as well. This was the perfect opportunity.

"I tell you, son, that woman across the hall from me is going to drive me insane. Just yesterday she invited me in and was buck-assed naked. Who invites a man to their home to seduce them? I certainly didn't expect it. My God, Blair, she wasn't a sight to behold, either."

Blair laughed so hard he nearly dropped the phone and ended up putting the phone on the cradle with the speaker on. He had his dad repeat the story, and, of course, he had to add enough more to it that Blair laughed again.

"You need a keeper, Allen. I think I might know of a couple of women that would love the job, too." He winked at Sapphire as she continued speaking to his dad. He wondered what his dad would think if he knew his future daughter-in-law had no blouse on and marks over her body where he'd taken her hard against this very desk.

"I don't know about too many women there, sweetheart. I wouldn't mind if one of them was you. Are you volunteering for the job?" His dad laughed. "I sure could use a pretty thing like you hanging on my arm."

"How about six of us? My sisters would love for you to come and live here with us. And Grandmother is hoping you'll come and help her by taste-testing her new recipes."

He waited for his dad to say something, anything, but he remained quiet. When Sapphire looked at him, he could see her fear. They'd all discussed this and were thrilled, really thrilled, about having him nearby. Sapphire said his name, and he heard his dad sniffle.

"Got something in my eyes. Hang on a bit there, girl. If you're going to be pestering me for quick answers all the time, I don't know about that." He blew his nose before he finally continued. "Moving in with you and that son of mine could cause more trouble than you think. He and I don't see eye to eye when it comes to women. What if he gets all hot and bothered when I play around with them sisters of yours?"

"How about if I keep him all hot and bothered too, and you'll be safe? I think you'll see that he's a changed man now." She leaned to the phone. "Please come and make our family complete, Allen. I'll make sure Grandmother bakes you an apple pie once a week."

"Sweetening the deal with pies, are you? Smart girl, you are. Could be that you'll keep that son of mine happy." Blair cleared his throat, and his dad laughed. "I know you're right there, but me and the new alpha is talking. Go and find yourself something to do. Damned if I could get you away from that desk of yours three months ago. Now you don't go anywhere near it."

"Because this one is very special to me. Not to mention I've found a whole new use for it." His dad blustered, and Blair laughed. "Will you move in here with us? There is more than enough room. And with the new construction going on, you can find yourself even more trouble to get into."

"I think I might take you up on that deal. Provided you understand that if I feel the need to leave, there won't be any hard feelings." Blair looked at Sapphire, and she nodded at his dad's stipulation.

"We'll be fine with whatever arrangements you want to make so long as if there's a problem as to why you're leaving you let us know what it is first. Maybe we can fix it a better way than you leaving us." He agreed. "Now, when can you move in?"

"I'm packing my stuff up now." Blair and Sapphire both laughed. "You two gonna be breeding soon? Would be nice to know when that happens, too. I just can't wait for a couple of fine young ones to bounce on my knee."

Blair looked at Sapphire. They hadn't talked about children, and he wondered if she wanted any. The sudden image of her swollen with his child made him sit up straighter in his chair. A child with this woman would complete him.

His dad told him he'd call him later and hung up. Blair watched Sapphire as she moved around the room picking up her tattered clothing and pulling on what she could find that was still intact. She tossed his shirt at him, and he pulled it on but didn't bother buttoning it. He needed a shower in the worst way.

"When do you leave?" She turned to him when he asked. "For Texas, when do you leave? Tonight or tomorrow, and do you plan to stay long?"

"Just one day if I can, and in the morning. Thad is sending his plane to pick me up." She sat down on his lap again. "He's thinking of moving his personal life up here. If he does, then we might want to think harder on telling him what we are at least. He might stumble upon something, and I'd rather he knew first so we didn't get shot to hell."

Thad liked to hunt and had asked them several times about the woods behind their house. Sapphire had told him that it was for their special use, and he'd taken it to mean that they romped through it naked on a daily basis. They did, but not like he thought they did.

"I'll see if I can figure out a way to work it in a conversation. How about we have him to dinner, and when he arrives, we're all wolves. You think that he'll try to have us stuffed and hung over his mantel like that moose he has there?"

Sapphire shivered. "I don't care to visit him in his home. It's like he's taken a zoo and had it stuffed. I hope to Christ he leaves that shit back in Texas. There is no way I'm ever going to feel good about going to his house with all those dead animals hanging around us."

Blair had had the same feelings and hoped the man would change once he moved here. His father had been a game hunter, and since it had been his house, both Blair and Sapphire hoped that he wasn't going to be a problem. He supposed time would tell.

Now he wanted to talk to her about children. He snuggled her into his arms and put his hand over her flat hard belly. Smiling, he thought again of children nestled there. This required tact as well as timing. He didn't want to upset her by coming across too strongly. Smiling, he had just the way to do it.

"So, how many pups would you like to have? I'm thinking a dozen." He grinned when she stiffened. "Maybe two, but no more than three dozen. That's my final offer."

About the Author

Kathi Barton, author of the bestselling series Force of Nature, lives in Nashport, Ohio with her husband Paul. In addition to writing full time Kathi likes to spend time with her eight grandkids, three children and three children-in-laws. She writes to relax and have fun.

Her muse, a cross between Jimmy Stewart and Hugh Jackman brings them to life for her readers in a way that has them coming back time and again for more. Her favorite genre is paranormal romance with a great deal of spice. You can visit Kathi on line and drop her an email if you'd like. She loves hearing from her fans. aaronskiss@gmail.com. Follow Kathi on her blog: http://kathisbartonauthor.blogspot.com/